HIPPOCRATES

THE ART AND THE OATH

Franklin Warsh

Dr. Franklin Warsh
London, ON, Canada
www.drwarsh.blogspot.com

Hippocrates – The Art and The Oath is a work of fiction. All incidents, dialogue, and characters, except some historical figures and events, are products of the author's imagination and are not to be construed as real. Where real-life historical figures appear, the situations, incidents, and dialogues, except those that are documented in history, are fictional and are not intended to depict actual events or to change the fictional nature of the work.

Hippocrates – The Art and The Oath / Franklin Warsh -- 1st ed.
ISBN 978-0-9958232-5-9

As to diseases, make a habit of two things — to help, or at least, to do no harm.

Hippocrates

War is a harsh teacher.

Thucydides

Map of the Athenian Empire ca. 450-430 BCE

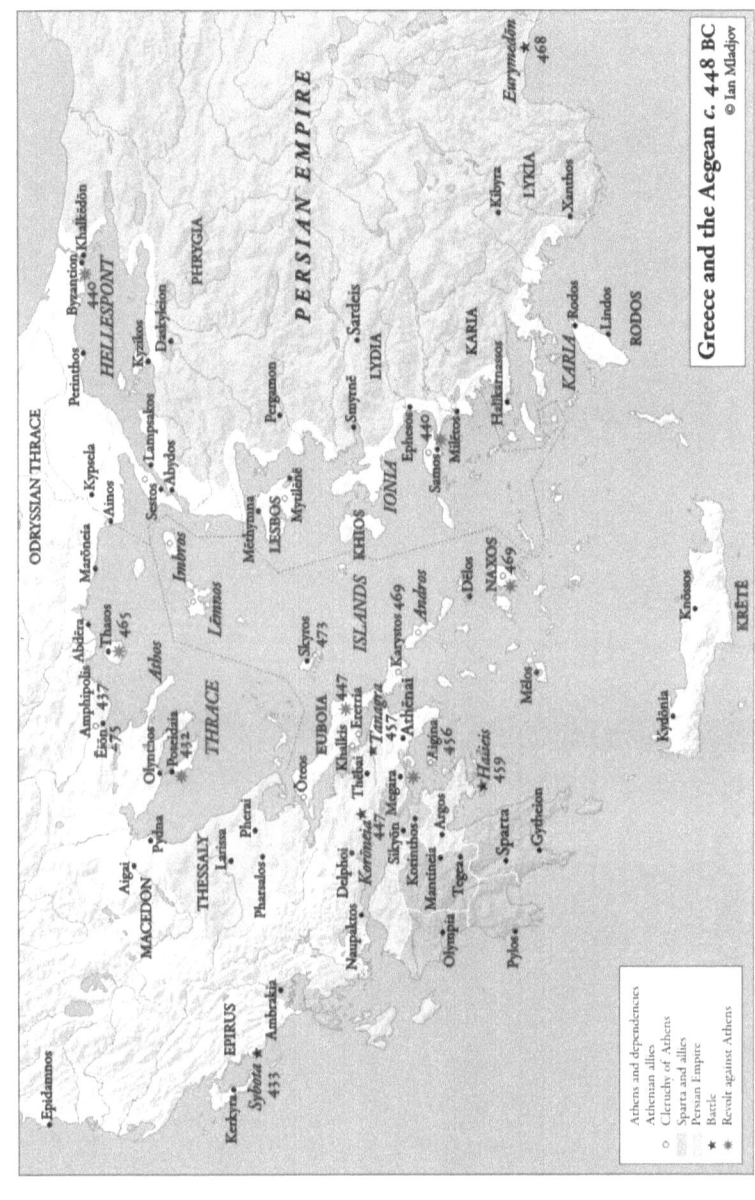

ONE

Athens, 431 B.C.E.

In the blazing glare of the midday sun, Pericles, son of Xanthippus, looked very much the god among men that he was in the eyes of his peers. It had been a long day for the Athenian citizens' assembly, gathered by the western foot of the Acropolis. There, on the Pnyx, the gently sloping hillside, gathered six thousand Athenians – his people – in rapt attention, hanging on the words of Athens' First Citizen.

As well the Athenians should have. Not because Pericles spoke in flowery rhetoric or poetic verse. He was calm, reserved, and measured in words, his voice sonorous but neither fiery nor soothing. No, Pericles had been the architect of a new Golden Age, a height of power Athens hadn't seen since the days of its legendary heroes. The temples of the Acropolis he beheld from the speaker's platform, the towering statue of Athena in the Parthenon, the walls to the port at Piraeus, the stockpiles of wealth paid in tribute...it was his vision, his gravitas, that made it all come to pass, not for his own glory but for Athens'.

It was only fitting that Pericles spoke last, as only his word had the authority to carry the day. On this day, the assembly gathered to vote on The War.

It had been fifty years since Athens and Sparta combined their forces to repel the Persian armies of Xerxes. Fifty years of uneasy peace, of proxy wars fought over colonial influence, of quashing rebellions, and of political schemes. Fifty years of the peerless Spartan army dominating the Peloponnesian peninsula. Fifty years of Athens' indomitable navy building an empire from the waters of the Aegean. With each city-state – each *polis* – its subjects and allies marshaling their resources, an aging peace treaty unraveling at the seams, the march to war had reached the point of no return.

Pericles spoke at length, answering the charges of Sparta's ambassadors, acknowledging the gravity of the decision at hand, but asserting his confidence in Athenian might. "It must be thoroughly understood that war is a necessity," he said, "but that the more readily we accept it, the less will be the ardor of our opponents, and that out of the greatest dangers communities and individuals acquire the greatest glory."

The Athenians and Spartans, and their respective allies, knew in their hearts this would be a long and bloody conflict, a war of attrition until one *polis* stood supreme.

What no one foresaw was the plague.

TWO

By afternoon, Hippocrates, son of Heraclides could do little but scratch out his morning's recollections on papyrus. As was the norm in summer, the marble columns lining the temple colonnade gleamed under the midday sun, blinding anyone venturing out from the shade. Resting against the tree where he discussed cases with his students each morning, he stroked his thick curly beard, reflecting on the patients, trying to connect symptom to cause, treatment to diagnosis. Their moans muffled by the din of cicadas, most of the patients would recover without incident, young and hale as they were. As for those that would not survive the summer, Hippocrates mulled over the progression of symptoms in his head. Had the patient arrived too late in the disease? Did he misjudge the timing of treatment? Was there something he hadn't tried, an Egyptian remedy escaping his memory this moment?

Hippocrates had stationed himself on his home island of Kos – or was it trapped himself – and the shrine to Apollo for three years now. Kos was an idyllic paradise, one of a string of islands in the eastern Aegean Sea dotting the southern coast of Asia Minor, and well removed from the hustle and politics of Athens and the mainland. His time at the temple was meaningful work, in service to the Art, and interesting on most days. It was only natural – no, duty – that he should tend to the sick in his father's footsteps, sharing discoveries with his cadre of students. Still, though duty to art and family and students came first, he yearned to travel the Aegean and beyond once more. Hiking and sailing from one exotic spot to the next, spellbound as much by the scenery as by the undiscovered secrets of the Art.

And this medical Art – **his** medical Art – was just in its infancy.

There would still be bones to set and wounds to cleanse, but disease and plague – the ailments that struck young and old, rich and poor – would no longer be accepted as the malevolence of an unhappy god. The air that one breathed, the miles that one walked, the balance of heat and cold...it was the physical world that affected man, just as man could affect his physical world.

It was the details that mattered: the history, the environment, the response to treatment, and the progress from onset to death. Every story was different, every patient unique, every subtle distinction the possible answer. Hippocrates recorded every observation, often before muttering a word, and impressed upon every student to do the same. With time, he said, every patient, every treatment, and every physician would be a tiny part of a sweeping body of knowledge, a mosaic of medical truths...a legacy to endure for centuries.

His scribbles were interrupted by the unceremonious thump of his friend and houseguest, Democritus of Abdera, plopping down on his left. "Lecturing, treatments, writing," said Democritus, "lecturing, treatments, writing. Don't you ever get bored of this, Asklepiad?" As a physician and alleged descendant of the mythical healer Asklepios, Hippocrates was accustomed to being addressed as *Asklepiad*.

The legend of Asklepios changed depending on which of his old relatives Hippocrates heard it from as a boy. As Hippocrates understood, Asklepios was the son of the Olympian god Apollo by a human princess. Depending on her identity, Asklepios' mother either died in childbirth or was slain by the goddess Artemis. Regardless of the mother's fate, Apollo rescued his demigod son to be raised by the centaur Chiron, who instructed the boy in the Art of medicine.

Asklepios eventually surpassed all others in his powers as a healer, including Chiron, gaining the power to restore the dead back to life.

"Not all of us can afford to be homeless philosophers," said Hippocrates.

"I'm not homeless," said Democritus. "I'm...itinerant. I'm exploring the larger Greek world, teaching bright young minds the art of reason and the nature of all things."

"Oh, well, excuse me," said Hippocrates. "Lecturing and writing are boring, says the 'itinerant' philosopher-teacher. And what is the nature of all things, again? That it doesn't exist? We're all...nothing, was it?"

"Gods, no. You're mistaking my philosophy for the nihilism of Gorgias," said Democritus, "who, by the way, is putting on yet another show for your patients."

"Is that why their moans seem louder this afternoon?"

"No, that's because you haven't had a drop of wine in days! You need to participate in the *symposium* tonight. I'll be debating Gorgias about my Grand Theory!"

"This is your idea that all things are made up of 'anthems'?"

"Atoms. Not anthems, atoms. There are atoms, and there is empty space. Nothing else."

"Oh yes, how could I forget? So Gorgias will be the one to argue that everything is really nothing?"

"It's more complicated than that, but if you wish to be vulgar that's not entirely inaccurate. Come on! I get to out-debate a sophist – no, **the** sophist! Gods, the party's taking place in your house! It's not like you'll find the peace to sleep. You must join in!"

"You need a drinking party as an excuse to debate? Are the rest of us expected to join in as part of the games?"

"No, no. I've arranged the entertainers. Flute girls for everyone, plus my darling Euthalia."

"You're bringing your whore to a *symposium?*"

"She's my consort, my *hetaera*! Whores are for slaves and barbarians. Besides, she's not left my company since we met months ago. Where else would she go?"

"Democritus, how much did you inherit when your father died?"

"Enough, I suppose. I don't stop to take count all that often. Why?"

"During my early travels, I learned of a disease described by the Egyptians: the urine turns sweet as honey, and once in crisis the patient can't stop drinking, and the breath grows rapid and deep." Hippocrates rolled up his papyrus, stood and brushed off the garment wrapped around his waist and over his left shoulder. Even under loose cloth, his physique maintained the athletic form honed by months of training at the gymnasium in his youth. "You, my friend, are pissing away your sweet fortune so quickly, it's a wonder your breath doesn't reach down to the Underworld. Come, let's save my patients from Gorgias' rhetorical nonsense." Considerably shorter and plumper, Democritus stood and followed suit.

The two strode passed the sacrificial altar, crossing to the *enkoimeterion*, the house of healing in the temple complex where the afflicted lay resting. It looked wrong, the sick strewn about the floor haphazardly, writhing on the hides of livestock offered in sacrifice. Someday I'll see a proper infirmary here, Hippocrates told himself.

As they hopped gingerly between the patients, Democritus pointed to a sweaty young man unable to find comfort on a white goatskin. "That one – with the bulging arm muscles – looks like he should be training for military service or the Olympiad. What's the matter with him?"

"Something brought by the change in seasons, changing the character of the water in the spring by the gymnasium," said Hippocrates. "I saw a series of similar cases in Thasos, all young men as well. Slight fevers, swelling and palpable lumps about the ears and jaw. Most recovered without treatment. This one remains ill with a painful, swollen testicle."

"Seriously? It hurts just to think about that."

"Hurts to think, says the philosopher."

They spied Gorgias of Leontini, fifteen years their elder, at the portico on the opposite end of the *enkoimeterion*, wagging a finger mid-air, lecturing at a pair of unresponsive youth on the ground.

"...gathered on the Attic plains, soaking under static rains. A plan formulated to perfection, perfected in its execution, executed as per formulation..." Gorgias spotted his friends from the corner of his eye and waved them over. "Democritus! Hippocrates! Join me here! Tend to these young men and lend me an ear! I remain powerless to raise either's consciousness!"

"Can I tell him?" said Democritus. "Please let me be the one to tell him."

"No," said Hippocrates. "You wouldn't want him unduly intimidated by your powers of observation, mere hours away from your master-versus-student drunken argument. It might give you an unfair advantage."

"Gorgias wouldn't mind. He's the first to say there's no such thing as unfair," said Democritus.

"Stop," said Hippocrates. "I'm still the physician here." The two joined their friend and tutor and embraced in a warm exchange of greetings.

"Hippocrates," said Gorgias, "tell me why these boys don't answer back. I'm giving my epideictic best, relating the chronicle of the victory at Plataea in my inimitable style." Gorgias the Sophist, master teacher of rhetoric and casual nihilist philosopher. He'd made a good living traveling around the Aegean and Mediterranean, peddling his theories and tutoring children of the affluent. Pay him enough, Gorgias would boast, and he'd coat your tongue in silver with the gifts of rhetoric he bestowed. He insisted on taking "only the worthiest" as students, which seemed at odds with the fact that many of his students were unrepentant delinquents, employing their Gorgias-given gifts to elude imprisonment. In truth, Gorgias could have handled twice as many students as he did, and made at least twice the money, were he not so enamored with putting his skills on display for anyone within earshot. He'd taught both Hippocrates and Democritus as boys and was enjoying the former's hospitality on Kos while the political tumult in Athens played out.

Hippocrates kneeled between the youths. One trembled, his eyes glazed over with tears, the other lay still and clammy with eyes closed. He snapped his thumb and forefinger beside each man's ear. Neither reacted to the noise. "Sadly, Teacher," said Hippocrates, rising, "we've been unable to communicate with them for days. Either they couldn't hear your glorious exhortations, or they're too delirious to respond. We gave each a suppository to help purge the disease, but neither has shown signs of response."

"Gods, they're young," said Gorgias.

"And too close together without a breeze to warm the air and aid with the discharge of humors," said Hippocrates. He tapped the papyrus against his hip. "Or maybe not. There's something I'm missing, I know it." Had he known no treatment existed for mumps virus, he'd have been spared many hours of rumination.

"Young and virile, hung and fertile," said Gorgias. "A tragedy of comic proportion were they to die." Hippocrates and Democritus rolled their eyes in unison.

The three men chatted until the day's heat began to dissipate and shadows returned to the temple courtyard, heralding the end-of-day bustle. Hippocrates' students checked over their respective patients once more, recording the volume and quality of excretions as measured by temple servants. The aspiring physicians relayed the pertinent details to Hippocrates, then returned to their quarters for supper and an evening of leisure.

Hippocrates scratched his students' findings onto scraps of broken pottery he kept in a chest by the entry portico to the *enkoimeterion* colonnade. With hours to go before the party Democritus had arranged, he'd pore over those notes for items of special interest and transcribe what seemed most important to papyrus for his permanent records. Before he could handle his clerical chores, however, he had one more patient to lay eyes on: his feisty young wife Theokleia.

His family estate was just over a mile from the temple, a pleasant walk if the sun wasn't oppressive. The house, a two-story structure built around an open stone courtyard, was impossible for a traveler to miss. Its entryway was marked by a mammoth Platanus, an Oriental plane tree that had been a signpost of Hippocrates' ancestral home for generations. It was under the Platanus that Hippocrates lectured to his students on the tenets of a physician's art, as his father and outsiders had done for him as a teen.

The ground floor was dominated by the *andron*, a large parlor that served as a party quarters for Hippocrates and other men of the household. The *andron* was also a serviceable place to crash if one guzzled too many cups of wine with too little food in one's belly. The house was abuzz with activity this evening, the household slaves fluttering about to fill oil lamps, ready refreshments, and arrange cushions on wooden couches. It was the final preparation for Democritus' *symposium*, a night of predictably drunken debauchery. Hippocrates had been to more than a few in his travels to the Greek mainland, and he knew one thing for certain. Once the wine flowed, all bets were off for any intellectual pursuits like debate to take place – most of the stimulation would be from music and sex. Not yet thirty, Hippocrates cared little for such misadventures, priding himself on keeping a clear head in the name of the Art.

He bounded upstairs towards the women's quarters. A nursemaid paced outside the door, a wriggling infant boy in her arms.

"I thought your fat friend had an appetite," said the nursemaid. "He's got nothing on your son, I tell you."

Hippocrates laughed, patting the baby on the head. "Hear that, Thessalus? You're making a boar of yourself on your nursemaid. Slow down, or you'll end up too stout for your potty!" He peeked into the room, seeing his wife covered with linens and apparently sleeping. "How's she been?"

"Same as yesterday," said the nursemaid. "Didn't touch a morsel of food. Kept some fluids down when the retching stopped, but not much."

"When you're done with the baby, prepare some *hydromel* for her, but minimally reduced through boiling. Keep it more dilute than normal, say six parts water to one part honey."

"As you wish, Asklepiad."

Hippocrates sat by his wife's side and touched her forehead. No fever, good. He gently lifted the bed linen. No sign of bleeding, better still.

"You're almost as loud as your son," said Theokleia, opening her eyes and making an effort to sit up. Even pale and disheveled, her figure of nineteen years and complexion were flawless. "Well, Master Physician, what's your opinion?"

"No fever or blood," said Hippocrates. He folded a cushion and positioned it to support her back. "Clearly the gods are pleased to see you pregnant again." A chuckle. "You're having ordinary daytime sickness, just somewhat worse than the norm and somewhat worse than I recall with Thessalus. A promising omen."

"I haven't felt this drained since I labored with Thessalus."

"The nurse will bring some dilute *hydromel*. It should help bring back some of your strength and appetite. If you keep it down, I'll sneak you some flatbreads and fruits from the symposium."

"Must you play host to an orgy with a sick, pregnant wife upstairs? The dancers, the flutes...is there no way to cancel and make amends with the guests?"

"Democritus is the host, we're just providing the venue. And I'll have the slaves hang a few spare tapestries to contain the noise, or at least keep it from waking you and the baby."

"And when the flute girls start making advances? Or that whore of Democritus? She seduces for a living. There's word the leader of the Athens is under the spell of a *hetaera*."

"Is this what you do with your day instead of taking fluids and rest? Fret about imaginary sexual exploits and trade gossip with the slaves? You know, most men expect their wives to spend their days at the loom."

"You've read nothing to me in weeks, nor spared a moment to share your stories from the temple! I'm bored! And beginning to wonder if you have eyes for another woman, or even a boy."

"What in Gaia's name has gotten into your head?"

"Don't get evasive on me! I know what men really think of women. Every monster in the old stories is female – the Gorgon, the Harpies, the Sphinx."

Hippocrates burst out laughing. "Now I know why most men won't let their wives leave the home or learn to read," he said. "I'd hate to see you act on these fantasies. You have nothing to fear. I've found ways to keep sober while the guests drink themselves silly. The entertainers won't bother a man who's sober...I'll be less likely to part with my spare coin. The boys I'll leave to Gorgias, thank you. And as for Euthalia? Never mind that Democritus pays her salary. There's not a wine in all of Greece that could get me to lie with her. Her bed's seen more action than the battlefields at Troy."

"Just be safe. Don't let your friends talk you into another wild sojourn on the mainland. I can't raise children by myself."

"By yourself, is it? Whose breast is feeding our son this very moment?" He sighed. "I won't go anywhere without consulting you, I promise. I have some records to transcribe before the party begins. Get some rest." He kissed Theokleia's forehead and jogged back down the stairs.

THREE

It was well into the night when two male slaves dragged Democritus from the house to vomit at the foot of the Platanus. His head spinning violently, Democritus smiled at his close friend and confidant, remnants of dinner trapped in the curls of his beard. "Tell me, Hippocrates," he slurred, "what disease am I struck with? Inspect my vomit and tell me!" He laughed in hysterics before throwing up once more and going limp.

"The light isn't adequate," said Hippocrates, "but the combination of undigested fruit and flatbreads would point to wine as the culprit."

"No! It's Apollo's arrow! I felt it, right in my ass!" hollered Democritus, taken with a giggling fit.

A clanging of bracelets announced the arrival of Euthalia, dashing from the *andron* to tend to her man. Threads of silk in her linen garment shimmered in the light of stars and oil lanterns, giving her buxom figure an ethereal glow that belied her chosen profession. "Is he okay? I saw him carried out of the parlor and was worried sick!"

"Nothing a little sleep and generous cup of *hydromel* can't undo," said Hippocrates, "but I don't think he'll be up for demonstrating his...athleticism this night."

"Even you know I'm much more than a bedmate to him," said Euthalia. "I'm his favorite student in philosophy, and a trusted interlocutor."

"Sadly, I don't anticipate he'll be putting his oral gifts on display tonight either," said Hippocrates with a smirk. "Best retire to your quarters and relish the night off." The *hetaera* fired a ghastly sneer and stormed back inside.

His wife out of commission with pregnancy sickness, and his sleeping quarters occupied with a degenerating party, Hippocrates felt compelled to make the uphill hike to the temple. Late as it was, the walk would be therapeutic, providing time alone with his thoughts and without the haze of daytime heat. He'd be exhausted later in the day, to be sure, but barring a crisis could spend the afternoon napping in the shade. Democritus would be hung over and in no condition to pester him, and with so many invalids as a prospective audience, Gorgias had more than enough ways to entertain himself in the daytime.

Even past midnight, the temple was a busy place. While those with minor ailments or fractures slept fitfully in the *enkoimeterion*, the wounded moaned in pain, and the severely ill trembled in fever or rigors, clinging to life. Temple attendants and slaves scurried about, uttering prayers, fetching water, or disposing of excrement. Hippocrates headed towards the bedsides of his patients suffering with complications of mumps. There at the feet of the sickest youth, the one suffering from the spread of the virus into his brain, stood a slender young girl, no older than fifteen, staring absently.

"What have you seen?" said Hippocrates.

The girl's gaze remained fixed. "He's been sweating," she said, "trying to fight the fever. The left side of him took with convulsions just moments ago. He's not opened his eyes nor noticed me."

"Nor will he," said Hippocrates. "It takes some time after a convulsion to regain consciousness. Not that it matters with this young man. He's been delirious for more than a day now."

"Will he die?" said the girl.

"Most likely. I've tried every remedy I know of, and his condition worsens by the hour. If he suffers more convulsions, I expect some form of bleeding will be close behind, heralding imminent death."

"The gods have cursed him."

"The gods played no part in this."

The girl swerved around, frightened. "Gods! You're the physician here, descendant of Asklepios! The Asklepiad Hippocrates!" She dropped to one knee and hung her head. "I'm sorry to be in your way."

"Young lady, I am neither your master nor the deity of this temple. I've been told that I'm descended from the god of healing, yes. My father believed that. But just as the gods are not the source of disease, I'm not convinced they're the source of healers either. Asklepios was a man of healing before he became a god of healing. Do stand up." The girl rose. "Now then...you've been standing here several moments without flitting about. Even in the meager light of stars and lanterns I can see your garment is too dirty for a temple servant. Who are you?"

"I don't know the name my parents gave me. I'm called Thratta in my master's household."

"You're a slave-girl from Thrace." Due north of the Aegean Sea, Thrace had a historically uneasy relationship with the Greek city-states. Thrace had provided the Persian King Xerxes with troops for his attempted conquest of the Greek world. Once the Persians were repelled for good, however, the Greeks accelerated their colonization of Thracian lands. The major appeal of Thrace was its abundance of two critical economic resources: silver and slaves. "I've been as far as Thasos off your coast but haven't ventured into Thrace itself. You've come a long way, though I suspect you're too young to remember your homeland. Who's your master?"

"I serve General Kleitos, *gymnasiarch* of Kos," said the girl. Men of wealth in the Greek world had a duty to fund public institutions. The gymnasium, where young men trained in competitive athletics, was a fixture in Greek communities, and its sponsorship fell to the *gymnasiarch*. "This man – that is, this youth is..."

"His son." Hippocrates was well acquainted with Kleitos and his family, socially and as a physician treating injuries suffered at the gymnasium.

"Yes. His son."

"Were you sent by his father to check on him?"

"No, I came on my own."

"What brings you here, then? Especially this time of night? Surely you'll be exhausted for your chores in the daytime."

"I could ask the same of you."

Hippocrates raised an eyebrow. "You could indeed. But I'm a free man, and a physician at this temple."

Thratta hung her head, unnerved and ashamed. "That was rude, disrespectful. Please don't tell anyone." She lifted her head, revealing eyes welled with tears. "When I heard about the party tonight, I thought I'd have time to see...to see him alone."

"That's fair. And I won't tell. I'm not supposed to be here either. If I were a proper host, I'd be drunk and engaged in something I shouldn't be this very minute. But it's amazing how a belly full of bread and being overly generous with a libation can keep you sober. Of course, no one will beat me for leaving a party. The same can't be said for a servant girl. You still haven't answered my question. Why come here alone this late at night?"

"I overheard Kleitos discussing his son's grave condition. The youth...he and I had been...close, in a way."

"Ah. So you have strong feelings for the boy?"

"No, it wasn't like that. He...he..." Her crying intensified, reflecting the unspoken truth of her life as a slave-girl.

"I understand." Hippocrates let a moment pass as the two stared in silence at the dying youth.

"May I ask you something?" said Thratta. "You said the gods play no part in sickness and cure. But the sick and the injured come here all the time, stay a few days, and return in perfect health. My master himself stayed here some months ago. He described visions of Asklepios and his daughter Panacea, cleansing his body of foul humors."

Hippocrates pointed to the opposite end of the *enkoimeterion*, where a priestly attendant knelt beside a woman asleep on sheepskin. "Do you see that woman being woken from sleep? She came with a complaint of fatigue, hard stools, and pain in the belly. She brought a votive, an offering of fruits and a plaque carved in relief, with the expectation that the gods would accept her gift and heal what ails her.

"Once the woman is the slightest bit awake, the priest will assume the 'voice' of a god. That voice will articulate a wish that the woman be cured, and the priest will pour some sort of remedy – likely a gentle purgative, but not necessarily – and let her fall back asleep. When she wakes, she'll recall a vision of the god in her dreams, have a rather large bowel movement, and leave in a state of bliss."

"I don't understand. How can a false vision make a sick person well?"

"It depends on how sick the person is to begin with. That woman's husband is playing host to a seafaring merchant, who no doubt arrived with all manner of exotic foodstuffs. All but the most rugged soldier will react to changes in the usual diet, women especially. Extra meals, fewer meals, something uncooked or overcooked...any of these will throw the body off kilter. Her symptoms would have proven to be short lived, whether or not she consulted the gods."

"So the temple healers are charlatans?"

"The remedies they administer often work, or there's at least a sensible rationale in trying. The votive offerings keep the temple attendants well fed. And the more cases my students and I see, the more knowledge we acquire in the name of the Art. All harmless, really. The so-called physicians that travel the countryside, peddling so-called 'cures' for drachmae – they're the charlatans."

Hippocrates spent some time explaining how the Art was practiced, how it was taught by his father and mentor, and his duty to pass on knowledge as it had been passed to him. However little she might have understood, Thratta was a captive audience. She also proved an eager assistant, fetching bandages and wound dressings with no sign of fatigue. An hour went by and Hippocrates found himself drifting.

"That's enough for me," said Hippocrates. "The partiers should all be asleep by now, so I can rest for a few hours before the sun comes up. You should get home as well."

"Thank you, Asklepiad," said Thratta.

Hippocrates took a few steps then paused. "Wait. I have a better idea. The streets aren't safe for a woman at night, especially with drunkards lurking about. I'll bring you to my home until morning. My house has more than enough room for one more girl to spend half the night. I'll have you escorted back to Kleitos at daybreak, with a report commending your dedication to his failing son."

Thratta wept in gratitude. "Thank you, Asklepiad. I am forever in your debt. Kleitos is an unforgiving master."

Hippocrates smiled. "Let me worry about that. Come, the stars are moving and you need all the rest you can get."

FOUR

"Now this is something you won't normally see on Kos," said Hippocrates, motioning for his students to gather around the patient, lying naked and spread-eagle on a makeshift table of wood planks. "As I've discussed time and again, the diseases we treat derive from an imbalance of humors – phlegm, blood, black bile, yellow bile. The imbalance arises by one of two paths. Either it originates with the environment, by changes in the air or in the water, or by our own hands...what we eat and drink or how much we exercise. Our job as physicians, as practitioners of the Art, is to understand these relationships and correct the imbalance. Apply cold to the hot, moisture to the dry, and so on, so that when the disease is at *crisis*, nature has the best chance at returning the body to health.

"Today we needn't worry about the cause of the patient's condition, because we already know it. This morning's lesson is a surgical one. We are going to go over the proper treatment of a fistula, a channel that develops from diseased skin around the anus into the rectum. Has anyone seen a fistula before?" The five students shrugged in silence. "Okay. Has anyone seen saddle sore before?" Silence again. "Hmm. Well, I suppose it's been decades since the war, so you just haven't been exposed to battlefield medicine.

"Rowers and cavalrymen are by far the most likely to develop fistulae. Long hours on horseback or at sea cause large volumes of blood to pool around the anus, stretching and weakening the surrounding flesh – saddle sore, as a horseman might say. Nikomachos here is a rigger on a merchant ship that began its journey in Korkyra, in the Ionian Sea to the northwest of the mainland. The wind wasn't enough to propel the ship, so Nikomachos went from rigger to oarsman for a long stretch of the voyage. All that sitting and rowing weakened his anal flesh.

"Once the flesh is weak and fragile, it only takes a slight injury – a fall, a sliver of wood – to create a pustule in the area. If your patient describes a pustule around the anus, or if you see one on exam, cut it open right away to let it drain. The last thing you want is the pustule to burst into the rectum and form a fistula. Unfortunately for Nikomachos, he didn't notice the problem until too late. The fistula expanded to the point that he noticed the fetid smell from contamination with flatus and feces."

And smell fetid it did, even in the open-air colonnade with a mid-morning breeze. Hippocrates made a habit of mouth-breathing as much as possible around the sick, but his students had yet to discover the best way to avoid foul odors. One youth looked absolutely peaked, another ashen and on the brink of passing out. Hippocrates signaled the most senior student to take the poor juniors aside to regain their composure. "Is that what minotaur shit smells like?!?" moaned the more alert of the two.

Hippocrates held up a garlic bulb. "The first step in the care of a fistula is measurement of its depth." He stuffed the garlic in the opening by the Nikomachos' anus, pushed it as deep as it would go, then plucked it out and held it up once more. A third student reeled from the blast of fetid air. "You can see by the fecal staining how big of a plug we'll need to help the area heal." He handed the garlic to a temple servant with directions to cut a patch of cotton. "We've already given our patient some medication beforehand. He's had three drinking cups of – can anyone recall the elixir?"

"Powdered fennel root, steeped for three days?" said the senior student.

"Four days," said Hippocrates, "plus some honey. Not

unpleasant to the taste, actually. The elixir is to be given on an empty stomach, after you've given a purgative. I don't advise wine for pain relief, despite the patient's discomfort." He accepted the cut cotton cloth from the servant and continued to demonstrate as he spoke. "You'll need to bleach the area clean with chalk. Then moisten your cloth in the juice of a milkweed and sprinkle it with grounds of roast orchid. Thread the cloth through the fistula until you can feel it on the inside the rectum…"

"Gods! That hurts!" screamed Nikomachos. "How soon can I have wine?!?"

"In due time," said Hippocrates, turning back to his students. "The cloth needs to stay in the fistula for six days. We'll fashion a small pessary – a plug made from the horn of an animal – then use it inside the rectum to keep the cloth in place. Nikomachos, you'll be able to remove the pessary as needed to move your bowels. At the end of the six days, we'll apply alum to the area to help dry it up. Then we anoint it daily with myrrh until the area is fully healed. Any questions?"

Hippocrates took delight in teaching the finer points of proctology. The Art was gaining traction in the Greek world, with physicians trained to look past deference to the gods. His contemporaries enjoyed popularity and wealth as they travelled, with success inflating their egos more than a little. Proctology was a terrific way to keep his students humble.

It had been two days since the *symposium*. As Hippocrates expected, the condition of Kleitos' son was grave. He never did regain consciousness and continued to suffer full-body seizures without warning. While the boy clung to life fiercely, death would almost certainly claim him within hours.

Hippocrates had dispatched Gorgias to accompany the slave-girl home, with an urgent summons for Kleitos to the temple. The General's home was a long walk from the temple. A child like Thratta could jog the distance in hours, but Gorgias was well past his prime. The trip would have taken most of the day, and it would be unthinkable for Kleitos to deny the travelling sophist dinner and a decent night's rest. Travel by night was possible, but unnecessary. Even if his son died in the meantime, Kleitos was a military man. He was unsurprised by death though not unmoved by it.

Gorgias arrived at the temple mid-afternoon, in advance of Kleitos and his retinue. He found Hippocrates scratching out the day's findings. "Hail, Asklepiad! Keeper of the Art, healer of the heart, scholar set apart, a..."

"Stop, Teacher," said Hippocrates, waving. "I presume Kleitos is not far behind?"

"That slack-jawed oaf travels with no less than five of his children at all times, and twice as many slaves and sycophants in tow," said Gorgias.

A growing murmur from the temple attendants signaled the General's arrival. His features scarred and weathered by military campaigns and advancing years, Kleitos was broad and muscular, projecting an aura of fear at those around him. Hippocrates greeted him by the temple's altar of sacrifice.

"General Kleitos, it's an honor," said Hippocrates.

"Where's the boy, and is he dead yet?" said Kleitos, his gaze penetrating.

"No, General, but I expect it anytime now," said Hippocrates. "His will is strong, but the disease has progressed beyond my knowledge."

Kleitos waved at his sons and servants, pointing them to the *enkoimeterion*. "His brothers will load him into the cart. We'll cremate him and bury the ashes on our lands. Thank you for your help, Asklepiad."

"I would be remiss if I didn't offer you the comfort of my home this night, General."

"A courteous offer, but a home with young children is no place for the dead. The boy needs swift passage to the afterlife, surrounded by family."

"There's one other thing, General."

"You want the slave girl instead of money as payment."

"How did you--"

"Please, Asklepiad. I have seen past fifty winters but I'm no fool. Why else would you send that long-winded ass to escort a slave, if not to negotiate for her on your behalf? I know what my son had been doing, and I know why she ran off to see him. What I don't know is what need you have for her."

"My wife is with child again, and quite sick. Our firstborn is proving a handful for the nursemaid. The girl will be a handmaiden to my wife."

"That's reason for another slave-girl, Asklepiad. I asked what need you have for *her*."

"They're the same reasons you're reluctant to let her go. She's perceptive, attentive, and duteous. I'd hate to leave my wife each morning in the hands of someone incompetent."

Kleitos thought in silence a moment, his expression unchanged. "Very well." He shooed Thratta to Hippocrates' side. "Gods willing, Asklepiad, this is the last child of mine that will need your services."

The General's children rolled the cart carrying his son into the main temple courtyard. Kleitos stared at the eyes of his eldest, eyes sunken into a face bruised from uncontrolled seizures, features wasting from dehydration. The youth's breathing was slow and rattling. He'll die before we're down the hill, thought Kleitos. He bellowed to the sky and tore at his hair, crying in the anguish no father should know. His younger boys tore their garments, joining their father in a sorrowful wail.

"I can only hope it's me buried next," said Kleitos. "A gods-cursed life, burying my first born." After a moment of solemn mourning, he composed himself. "Have you been summoned yet, Asklepiad?"

"No. Summoned where?" said Hippocrates.

"The Athenians and Spartans are at war. Even now, Pericles' emissaries sail the Cyclades, marshalling resources and men. They'll have need of your skills sooner or later, Asklepiad."

"Thanks for the warning. And condolences to your family." Without a word, Kleitos and his entourage left the temple behind.

Once the General faded from view, Thratta kneeled and bowed her head. "I owe you my life, Asklepiad," she said. "I will serve your family tirelessly."

"Please," said Hippocrates, "I have no need to work you to the bone. We'll hold a ceremony welcoming you to the family tonight. But the name – Thratta – it's meaningless. You're in need of a proper name if you're to live under my roof."

"Thratta is the only name I've ever known."

Hippocrates stroked his beard in thought. "How about taking the name 'Thaïs'?"

The girl blushed. "It's lovely. What does it mean?"

Hippocrates grinned. "Bandage. Or if you prefer, bond."

FIVE

As she stepped across the threshold of Hippocrates' stately home, the young slave found herself showered in dried fruits by the giggling baby Thessalus, held high overhead by his father. The other household servants sung a cheerful tune.

"Welcome Thaïs!" said Hippocrates, beaming. "You are now *oiketes*, part of the household." Thaïs bowed demurely. "Now, now. None of that. We'll be putting you to work in the morning. For tonight, you'll be the family's guest at dinner." Hippocrates handed his son back to the nursemaid.

Democritus pushed through the wall of servants to stand behind Hippocrates. "That's a bit odd, don't you think?" he whispered. "She's a child and a slave. You're treating her like an ambassador from the mainland."

"I've been accused of the same from my wife for the hospitality I extend to a homeless man and his bedmate for hire," said Hippocrates.

"That's hurtful, Asklepiad," said Democritus. "I'm a man of wealth and honor."

"And here I thought you were a man of 'atoms'." The two friends laughed heartily. "Come, the feast awaits." As the group headed to the dining table, Hippocrates leaned into Thaïs' ear. "Sit next to Gorgias rather than Democritus, young lady."

"So as not to offend Democritus' companion?" whispered Thaïs.

"Euthalia? Oh, offend her all you like," said Hippocrates. "No, it's your first night in my home, and I'd hate to see you flee on account of my good friend's...shall we say, 'wandering appendages', from whatever part of him they arise."

Hippocrates waited for his wife and guests to settle. Space was tight around the table, a reflection of how rare it was for him to host a dinner or eat with a crowd. Most nights Hippocrates ate quickly, either alone or with Democritus, and returned to his work by the light of a lantern. Kos was a sail away from any *polis* in Asia Minor, and the Greek mainland seemed the other end of the world. Important visitors rarely bothered to stay with him, unless those visitors brought a sick relative for a physician's attention at the temple.

Servants handed out drinking mugs around the table and presented Hippocrates with a shallow silver bowl for mixing wine with water. A female servant poured wine from a pottery jug, decorated with red and black patterns and an illustration of a centaur and boy, while a male servant poured a larger volume of water to match. "This wine jug is the prize of my potteries," said Hippocrates, "a gift from the General Cimon to my father. It depicts the centaur Chiron tutoring Asklepios, my forebear and originator of the Art. Normally I reserve its use for when I deem a student is ready to practice on his own.

"However, I often reflect on the tale of how Asklepios came to his divinity. Here was a healer, slain by the god Zeus for raising the son of Theseus back from the dead. Why? Not because the dead youth was evil. No, Asklepios was killed because he took a king's ransom in gold in exchange for his services."

"I thought it was because Hades was worried he'd run out of dead people," said Democritus. "And Zeus brought Asklepios back from the dead and put him among the stars to quell a hissy-fit by Apollo."

"Always raining on the moment," sighed Hippocrates. "The story begins and ends in a hundred ways. My point, however, was that healing is not an act to be punished, but greed in the name of healing is. Today I was reminded of a core tenet of the physician's Art, a precept I make a point of sharing with my students: where there is love of man, there is love of the Art. Some patients recover their health simply through their contentment with the goodness of the physician. As the newest member of our household, Thaïs, I hope that you will recover your health and contentment, simply by the warmth of my home." Hippocrates poured a libation onto the ground beneath him. "For the gods."

"For the gods," answered those at the dinner table, savoring their first swig of wine. The meal was indulgent, though not decadent: servings of chicken with rosemary, barley flatbread with honey, and a bountiful course of vegetables with dried fruits. Even the slaves were afforded breaks to feed themselves. Generous mugs of wine helped stretch the merriment from evening into night.

Democritus pounded the table. "Gorgias, we did not have our debate the night of the *symposium*. I say we have it right here and now," he said, winking at his companion.

"No!" said Hippocrates. "No philosophy! My tree can't handle more vomit."

"Fine," said Democritus, "but we need some entertainment!" He reached down and squeezed Euthalia's curvaceous behind. She retorted with a playful light slap on the cheek. "Gorgias, a story from your many travels!"

"Are you going to silence me after three sentences like you usually do?" said Gorgias.

"By the gods," said Hippocrates, "you have our attention as long as you wish!"

The festivities moved to the *andron*, where Gorgias picked up a dusty, out-of-tune lyre and plucked a few random notes. "Shall I tell the tale in verse?"

"Oh, get on with it!" said Euthalia, snuggling into Democritus' arms.

"Alright," said Gorgias, "I've got one I know you'll like, Hippocrates: my encounter with the warrior women of Sarmatia!

"Sing, O Muse, and tell the tale,
Of distant lands I reached by sail,
Past Lemnos, Imbros, and Chersonese,
Through Hellespont to Propontis seas,
Past Bosporus, where Aeolus stilled the wind
'Til our prayers did the curse rescind,
To Pontus Euxeinos, the Unfriendly Sea,
Sailing ever north, 'gainst the dread in me-"

"Hey, Admiral!" said Democritus. "Do you ever make it off the gods-cursed boat?"

"Silence yourself, you babbling, bumbling boor!" said Gorgias. "Now, where was I?

"Cross northern straits to the Maeotian Swamp,

And mouth of the Tanais, where Amazons stomped,

The lands of Sarmatia, a Scythian realm,

Where barbarian hordes might fast overwhelm

An expedition like mine, to explore and to teach,

Armies to protect me worlds beyond reach.

We landed the boat and did scouts dispatch,

While oarsmen and boat-hands sought fish to catch.

Once on land I turned an eye,

Beheld the flora, when I did espy

A charge of hoofbeats, like none before,

Ten cavalry? Twenty? Many more?

Before I even took a breath,

I was face-to-face with certain death.

An arrow pointed at my heart,

I felt all courage fast depart—"

"Since when do you have courage?" said Euthalia.

"Since I bore witness to your fat friend's phallus!" said Gorgias. "Now let me finish!

"In disbelief I lifted eyes,

And spotted much to my surprise,

Not mighty men atop the steeds,

Prepared to do the lethal deed,

But women – virgins! Like Artemis fair,

Of muscular build and close-cropped hair.

I dropped to ground, bowels nearly loose,

Murmuring prayers to aegis-bearing Zeus,

Begged, 'Fair Sarmatians, indomitable race,

I beseech your mercy, as I make haste

To leave your lands and go back home,

Send me not to lie in tomb.

I am but a teacher, a mere man of words,

No butcher of men, nor slayer of herds.'

They lowered their bows and put away spear,

Stepped down from horse and drew me in near,

Speaking in dialect I barely made out,

Ordered me 'follow' and recall my scout.

We walked on through marshes, thicket and swamp,

Came to a village, no triumph nor pomp

Announced our arrival. The girls did dismount,

And led all their horses to drink from a fount,

Cast off their breastplates and laid down their arms,

Unfixed their tunics and caused me alarm,

For each of the girls, unmarried and chaste,

Had only one breast 'tween neckline and waist."

"Oh, come on!" said Democritus. "There are no such people. Why in Gaia's name would an entire people remove young a woman's breasts? And send these girls on horseback armed?!? Is this a wager you made with a student, that you could get a room full of people to believe folk-tale nonsense?"

"Hippocrates, care to tell him?" said Gorgias smugly.

Hippocrates chuckled. "The Sarmatians don't remove the right breast of their girls, but they do apply a hot copper to it. The copper burns the flesh of the breast and halts its growth. It enables the right arm and shoulder to develop strength on par with a man's, or at least strength enough to pull a bowstring and throw a javelin. I've heard the story – mind you, without the part about the threat on Gorgias' life – from my mentor Herodicus."

"To disfigure young girls! What about marriage and childbearing? Don't the men frown upon brides whose bodies are marred?" said Theokleia.

"Apparently, the girls remain virgins until they've slain three of the enemy," said Hippocrates. "After that, it's good-bye cavalry and good-bye chastity...marriage and normal domestic life, so we're told. I imagine the glory of knowing your wife put an arrow in the heart of an enemy soldier more than makes up for the scars in the eyes of a husband. Besides, the procedure is only done on the daughters of families with status. No doubt the Sarmatians will have peasant women as nursemaids and such."

"I'd never let anyone do that to my body," said Euthalia.

"It would make foreplay go smoother," said Democritus. "No more choosing which side to start with."

"It's been a while for me," said Gorgias, "but don't you still have to choose between the front and the back?"

"I'm going to be ill," said Theokleia. "Please excuse me, dear husband and guests. I'm going to rest."

"I'll see you before I retire tonight," said Hippocrates. "If you're awake or at least rousable, I have something to discuss." He motioned for Thaïs to escort Theokleia to the woman's quarters, giving both girls a warm good-night embrace.

"I'll leave you men to your politics and philosophy too," said Euthalia. She whispered something in Democritus' ear to put a mischievous grin on his face and left the men alone in the *andron*.

"Gorgias," said Hippocrates, "the General said that war's finally broken out between Athens and the Peloponnese."

"It has," said Gorgias. "The conflict's been building since I was a young man, if not all the way back to the time of the war with the Persians. Sparta's leading the united confederacy of the Peloponnesians. They've got everyone on the peninsula siding with them, except Argos that's sworn neutrality for the time being."

"The Spartans are vicious on the battlefield," said Democritus, "fearless and more disciplined than any army in Greece. How does Athens hope to beat them?"

"Kleitos was convinced that the Athenians wouldn't engage on land," said Gorgias. "Perhaps they're hoping for a quick naval campaign. Kleitos was a man of few words. Why the interest, Hippocrates?"

"Something the General said," said Hippocrates. "My 'skills would be needed'."

"I know that wistful look," said Democritus.

"With all that wine, I'm surprised you can see your hand before your face," said Hippocrates. "But it's been three years since I last traveled off Kos for any length of time. My senior student is more than capable of covering for me at the temple. Theokleia's with child…"

"…and you've got the itch," said Democritus.

"And I've got the itch."

"So we'll be catching a ride to the Piraeus with that fellow whose anus you stuffed with onions?" said Democritus.

"Garlic," said Hippocrates, "but no, I'll not leave that soon."

"Why leave at all?" said Gorgias. "You've built a great home, a great life, with a great income. Kos is peaceful, beauteous, and bountiful. Go to war, and either Athens will bankrupt you or Sparta will butcher you. Either way, it's a miserable trip to Asphodel in the afterlife."

"Life is short," said Hippocrates, "and the Art long. Surgery on battlefield wounds is part of the Art. My duty is neither to Athens nor Sparta, but to the Art. Where I end up in the afterlife is immaterial."

"You can be as stiff as a dead man's phallus," said Democritus.

"I wouldn't know," said Hippocrates. "How would you?" The three men shared a boisterous laugh. "So that's that. I'll get the household and temple in order. We depart before summer's end."

Thaïs knelt as Hippocrates entered the room to the sounds of his wife resting soundly. "She sleeps, Asklepiad," whispered Thaïs. "She lay down as soon as we came upstairs. Shall I rouse her?"

"No," said Hippocrates. "it can wait until morning or after I take my evening meal."

Thaïs rose. "Your household is so tranquil, Asklepiad. Even the slaves seem unbothered by their lot in life."

"And what about you? Are you...bothered by your lot?"

"Not any longer, Asklepiad. You've freed me from pain, given me food, shelter, and now purpose. Your wife is so beautiful, as is your son. I can't wait to meet your next child...or, did you intend for me to work at the temple?"

"There's time to decide that. For the time being it will depend on where we need an extra pair of hands." He spied his wife's eyelids fluttering. "Thaïs, I need to get an hour or two of transcription done before I retire for the night. I'll ask you to see that the lanterns downstairs are refilled with oil." Thaïs nodded and bowed out of the room. Hippocrates ran a hand through his wife's hair. "We're alone. You can open your eyes."

"No fooling the great Hippocrates," said Theokleia. "So what's this thing you needed me to discuss with me?"

"War's broken out between the mainland powers."

"Have you been called to fight?"

"No, and I can't imagine I would be. But Kos is part of the Athenian-led league and pays a generous tribute. It's a matter of time before Athens comes asking for more."

"What does that mean for us? Is there a problem with the household accounts?"

"No, not at all. Athens will need muscle more than money, especially oarsmen for their warships and laborers. We might need to find replacements if we lose some of the farmhands, but those are minor concerns."

Theokleia sat up and held her husband's hand. "So what's the worry?"

"I'm going to be needed. There will be broken bones to set, wounds to debride, cures to discover…healing is a matter of time, but also sometimes a matter of opportunity. Medical practice is not just theories, but experience combined with reason."

"And you crave the experience that will only come with war?"

"It's my duty to the Art."

"What about your duty to household? To your children? To the wretched that seek your care at the temple?"

"I've kept records of everything I've discovered caring for people at the temple. I've taught my students everything they need to continue my work, including how to keep records of their own. The patients at the temple will be well served in my absence."

"And us? Your family? I recall you promising to consult with me. This isn't much of a consultation." Hippocrates was a loving husband, but Theokleia sensed the futility in her pleas.

"I've travelled before and the household ran itself," said Hippocrates, disregarding the challenge to his authority. "Thessalus has yet to speak his first words. Before long you'll be awaiting labor, hardly able to stand, let alone spend time with me."

"But the boredom when you're gone!"

"I'll tell you what. It will be weeks before we leave. I'll ask Gorgias or Democritus to teach you the basics of writing. You can write down every bit of gossip you hear while I'm away, and I'll keep a journal of every time I slice a head off a hydra. We'll compare stories when I return."

"You're not funny! I'll miss you," Theokleia sighed.

"And I you," said Hippocrates, "very much." He kissed his wife deeply, and they made love in the calm of the night.

SIX

Onesimos despised the blistering heat the Nile Delta, but business was business. If he had to make his way around Naucratis covered in dust from the mud-brick temples and wearing a peasant's head covering, so be it. He had poured every spare drachma into refitting the old ship for human cargo. Still, if the rumors out of Athens were true, it was a pittance compared with what he stood to earn in the coming years.

Naucratis was the most important trading post in the Delta, at least so far as the Greeks were concerned. Not quite fifty miles inland from the coast, it was a thriving city on the Canopic, the westernmost arm of the Nile. Every port in the Aegean lay due northwest from the mouth of the Canopic.

Even an idiot could navigate a boat from Naucratis to Greece, and the constant traffic along the shipping lanes meant for limited exposure to piracy.

There were stories, even fables, surrounding the Greek presence in Egypt. Some were pure nonsense – a courtesan from Naucratis, a lover of the fabler Aesop no less, had ordered one of the pyramids built. Others, tales of pirates and mercenaries of Greek blood, fighting for or against this or that Pharaoh, probably had some degree of truth. The Egyptians were better record keepers and probably had the story straight, but who could make sense of their drawings?

A sonorous humming voice broke Onesimos' concentration.

"And down I set the cushion
Upon the couch that she,
Relaxed supine upon it,
Might give her lips to me."

Onesimos grinned as the song grew louder behind him. "You're singing Sappho now? I didn't think an Egyptian jackal would have use for Greek songs and poems."

"Beauty in verse and melody knows no king or nation," said Kenamon. "Besides, you throw a fit every time I sing of Rhodopis, blush-cheeked courtesan..."

"Your singing is awful," groaned Onesimos, "but it's good to see you, my friend."

"And you," said Kenamon, embracing his longtime merchant partner. Son of an emissary-advisor to the Pharaoh, Kenamon had been born and raised in Naucratis. Growing up in a trading hub had made him proficient in Greek, able to grasp if not articulate some of the dialect subtleties of the various Greek city-states. But the etiquette and ritual of the Pharaoh's court bored him to tears as a youth, dragged as he was from one royal audience to another. Against his father's wishes he struck out as a merchant, first in pottery, then slaves. Trade in pottery demanded high-interest loans as security, in case the cargo was damaged in shipping. If a slave drowned in the sea or was stung by a scorpion, you could always find another without looking too hard. "Come, let's step away from the crowds to talk business."

The north of Naucratis was dominated by the Hellenion, a multipurpose shrine built by the coastal city-states on the eastern Aegean. Surrounding it were older temples built by Greek mainlanders, principally in honor of Hera and Apollo. Shops and modest mud-brick homes belonging to merchants and craftsmen spread outward from the temples, built tightly together on dirt roads laid out more or less in a grid. Onesimos had waited for his friend by a clothier's shop, and the two walked south, making small talk until they reached the back of a workshop that molded glazed scarabs and other inexpensive jewelry.

"So what have you got for me?" said Onesimos.

"Just as you asked, thirty men, all able-bodied," said Kenamon. "My men raided a village in northern Kush, just beyond the first cataract of shallow waters on the Nile – Aethiopia, I believe the Greeks call it. It's a kingdom run by a tyrant. Outside the cities Kush is a land of peasants and laborers. None of them stood a chance when my men attacked. If you're interested I've got some women and children as well..."

"Do with the women and children as you please. My boat will be full enough with the men and provisions. I'm picking up a load of marble on Naxos before landing at Athens. Last thing I need is more mouths to feed."

"Where will you stow the men?"

"Stow them? They'll be my oarsmen until I hoist sail. The drunks in my crew can stay in Naucratis. Let them spend their coin on your whores."

"Why only the men?"

"Kenamon, the entire Greek world is about to erupt in war. Athens has ordered the construction of hundreds of warships, all with three banks of oars. They'll need to haul every piece of timber in Thrace to build a fleet that size, and mine every ounce of silver they can find to pay for it.

"The Athenians, if you can believe it, also boast that only their citizens will man the oars. Please...not with a fleet that vast, they won't. The men of property spend too much time on philosophy to sully themselves with hard labor, and the peasants will be needed to pick every last olive on the mainland before the Spartans lay waste to it all.

"Slaves, my friend – muscle – will be the indispensable resource in the months and years ahead. I'll take this first group to the Piraeus to get a feel for what price the market will bear. In the meantime, tell your thugs to sharpen their daggers. They'll have plenty of work by the next time we see each other."

SEVEN

As the autumn equinox approached, Hippocrates had put his household in order and readied himself for the journey away from home. Gorgias and Democritus were leaving Kos as well, elated by the chance to ply their teachings in the bustling Athenian *agora*.

Hippocrates had gathered his students this cloudless morning by the Platanus at his estate for a final exhortation and oath-swearing ceremony, and to field last-minute questions before he left the temple patients and people of Kos in their care. One by one, each new physician was ushered to lay a hand on a sculpture of the Rod of Asklepios – a bronze serpent wrapped around a staff of marble – and swear a sacred oath to the Art.

"...While I continue to keep this Oath unviolated, may it be granted to me to enjoy life and the practice of the Art. But should I trespass and violate the Oath, may my practice and life's pleasure be forfeit!"

"Congratulations all of you!" said a beaming Hippocrates. "Much like the Art, the tenets of the Oath are still a work in progress, imperfect but inviolate. Someday I'll get the wording just right. But a solemn oath it remains, in witness of all the gods of healing. To you that have sworn it today, I am proud to call you my brothers. You juniors, whose skills and experience have yet to reach full maturity, I leave you in my brothers' capable hands. Whenever I might return to Kos, or encounter you in my travels, it will be your knowledge and your expertise that educates me. No teacher of the Art could ask for more." The fledgling doctors gave Hippocrates a standing ovation. "Now, before I take leave and present you with a gift of sorts, are there any lingering questions?"

A junior student raised a hand. "Teacher, are there general rules to keep in mind around a patient's diet restriction during an acute disease?"

"You must form a particular judgement of the patient," said Hippocrates, "whether he will support the diet until the peak of the disease, or the disease will give way and become less acute. However, for extreme diseases, extreme methods of cure, including diet restriction, are most suitable."

A second junior raised a hand. "Teacher, I attended the bedside of a frail elderly man. He presented with catarrhs, inflammation of mucous membranes, but no fever or coryza or other symptoms. How do I treat him?"

"Symptoms like catarrhs and coryza in very old people don't go together as they do in the young. You'll discover that with more experience. Treat in accordance with your best judgement."

A senior student spoke next. "We had a patient at the temple with unexplained pain in a single limb. There had been no accident or wound to explain the pain, nor was there any fever or purging to suggest a bodily disease. Still, the patient reported severity of the pain as extreme. Not even intoxication with undiluted wine would control it."

"I've seen that before," said Hippocrates. "The phenomenon is uncommon, but very real. Approach such cases with extraordinary care. Many that have a painful affection in the body, and are sensible of the pain beyond what concurs with your judgement and experience, are disordered in intellect."

"Do you mean they're mad?" asked the senior.

"Not unless they've acted mad, no. But there is often melancholy, an excess of black bile that these patients suffer from. Anything else?" The students nodded in understanding, and none raised a hand.

"Wonderful, because I have something of a parting treat for you!" said Hippocrates. "As I have said on many occasions, medicine possesses all the qualities that make for wisdom: modesty; reserve; sound opinion; judgment; quiet; pugnacity; purity; knowledge of the things good and necessary for life; freedom from superstition; and so on. But the Art also demands that the physician be able to sell that which cleanses. Needless to say, that is a very different skill from those which you've sought my tutelage for. Fortunately, that skill – persuasion through oratory – is more easily attained than the artistry of a physician."

"Easily attained?!?" said Gorgias, who'd been standing just inside the Platanus' blanket of shade.

"But not cheap," Hippocrates retorted. "So as my farewell gift to you, I offer a lecture from Gorgias here. You've no doubt seen him around the temple or tutoring other youth in recent months. He is my friend and mentor in sophism, the philosophy and art of rhetoric. A great physician is a great talker, and your education is not complete until you've learned to talk from the master himself."

Gorgias strode to face the young physicians to a measured round of applause. "Thank you, thank you. And thank you, Hippocrates. This is such an honor for me, to appear before such young physicians, healing magicians, masters of the Art, champions of the heart. I come before you not to lecture, but to share; not to frighten, but to enlighten; not to..." Gorgias carried on for another few minutes in florid monologue, with no clear lesson evident.

A senior trainee finally raised a hand. "Master Gorgias, I beg your pardon."

"No bother, young man," said Gorgias. "Never would I dampen the dynamism of an intrepid interlocutor. Do introduce yourself."

"I am called Eryximachus, Master."

"Well met, Eryximachus. Present your pressing query, and no need to address me formally."

"Thank you, Gorgias," said Eryximachus. "Would it be unseemly if I asked that you come to a point?" Hippocrates let out an audible snicker, a snicker drowned out by a boisterous guffaw from Democritus.

"Ah," said Gorgias, "that distinctive doubt around the power and wizardry of words! Tell me, Eryximachus, have you ever had a patient refuse a purgative?"

"Of course," said Eryximachus. "Even Hippocrates will have patients that disregard his counsel."

"Indulge me in a story, then. My brother, a physician himself and sometime mentor to your Hippocrates, one day came upon a patient who badly needed a purge but refused to heed a physician's advice. My brother, well acquainted with the myriad talents of my tongue..."

Hippocrates nudged his elbow into a giddy, giggling Democritus. "Not a word," murmured Hippocrates, "Not a word."

"I'll shut up on one condition," murmured Democritus. "Admit it...you put him up to this for your own entertainment, not for their education."

"Me? Of course not," said Hippocrates. "But I've always believed the physician must have at his command a certain ready wit. Dourness is repulsive to both the healthy and the sick."

"Plus you knew I'd enjoy this," said Democritus.

"Plus I knew you'd enjoy this," said Hippocrates.

"...so you see," said Gorgias, carrying on with his lecture to Eryximachus, "without rhetoric at your ready, dialectic at your disposal, how would you get that patient to take a noxious purgative?"

"Easily," said Eryximachus. "The symptoms get worse, so the patient finally decides to listen." Democritus and Hippocrates doubled over in laughter, and even Gorgias chuckled at the practical joke he's been an unwitting victim of.

Hippocrates waved an end to Gorgias' demonstration and embraced his former teacher in a show of warmth. He spent the next hour or so extending best wishes to his students individually, reiterating his confidence in each of them. When the group dispersed, Hippocrates, Democritus, and Gorgias retreated to the andron for a midday meal and wine.

"I've heard back from my friend and former student Polus," said Gorgias. "He has more than enough space in his house for all of us, the women included."

"Women?" said Democritus. "I thought it was just Euthalia with us. Hippocrates' wife is with child. She doesn't belong in Athens, at least not while the country's at war."

"Euthalia and the girl will be joining us in Athens," said Hippocrates. "Thaïs."

"She's not staying to help Theokleia with the delivery?" said Democritus.

"She probably should," said Hippocrates, "but I need a servant to keep my writings and effects in order. Having a female with me makes it easier to escape the parties you'll be attending night after night. You'll keep an eye on her until my arrival in Athens, Gorgias?"

"Of course," said Gorgias, "but are you not joining us? If you stay for Theokleia's labor, you'll be well into winter, won't you? Even the greediest merchants won't brave the winter seas. We wouldn't see you 'til spring at the earliest."

"You might not see me until spring anyways," said Hippocrates. "I'm going to Potidaea. Kleitos is leading an infantry contingent from Kos and Rhodes to reinforce the Athenian siege."

"What does that have to do with you?" said Democritus.

"I can't master battlefield medicine from inside the walls of Athens," said Hippocrates.

"You're risking your neck," said Democritus, "and your family's security."

"I'm not marching in the line," said Hippocrates. "I'm there strictly for the medical work – cauterizing wounds, setting fractures, amputating gangrenous limbs. If I can arrange it, I'll even offer my services to Potidaea as well. The Art knows no allegiance to any one faction or *polis*."

"Someday your principles and your work ethic are going to land you in a whole goat herd's worth of shit, my friend," said Democritus. "Just make it to Athens alive and in one piece."

"I will," said Hippocrates. "If I can handle homeless philosophers as houseguests, surely open combat can't be any worse." The friends drank their wine with a hearty laugh, doing their best to quell their dread of the war.

EIGHT

Hippocrates struggled to keep his gaze fixed at the beach on the horizon, doing what he could to keep from vomiting. He'd been at sea many times over the years, even in choppy waters, but those voyages had been aboard merchant ships with wide berths. He now stood on the forecastle of a trireme – a warship, albeit an old one – propelled by three banks of oars and built for ramming an enemy vessel. Since the Persian war fifty years earlier, the trireme had been the ubiquitous vessel of naval power in the Greek world. The newer ships were more imposing, built with a larger deck to carry a contingent of soldiers should an enemy ship be oriented for boarding. This trireme from the island of Rhodes had, until now, been relegated to training oarsmen in Athens' tribute states in the southeastern Aegean. But in a pinch, she could be used to secure port traffic and ward off pirates.

In a narrow strait, with a properly drilled crew, even an old trireme could zip through the water and ram another ship's hull into kindling. Unfortunately for Hippocrates, the northwestern Aegean was anything but a narrow strait, and the oarsmen on this ship were anything but properly drilled. The oarsmen, reservists from the Kos and Rhodes citizenry joining the expedition to Potidaea, strained to synchronize their strokes. The boat struggled to hold course, even navigating in the relative calm of gulf waters. The most moderate of broadside waves caused the ship to teeter near the point of capsizing, and seasickness caused Hippocrates to expel at least one meal a day.

Kleitos strode up beside him, unfazed by the motion of the boat. "We'll be landing soon, Asklepiad. The encampment is just south of the isthmus. A few hours on dry land and you should be good to eat."

"Thank you, General," said Hippocrates. "I'm sure I'll be fine."

"Don't forget to breathe," said Kleitos.

"I beg your pardon, General?"

"We shallow the breath when we're seasick, thinking we're less likely to vomit. It's a faulty reflex. Deep breaths of fresh air are a better cure than staring dead ahead. It's why the oarsmen don't toss every morsel of food they eat...they need to take in all the air they can get."

"I'll remember that, General. Thank you. May I ask what the plan will be once we land?"

"No idea. What, you think the Athenians are willing to share their master plans with a galley of backwater islanders? Athens demands troops, we bring them troops. You can do as you wish, Asklepiad. Just make sure you're facing the blunt ends of the spears when you do it." Kleitos gave Hippocrates a hearty slap on the back and walked away to talk with the crew.

Potidaea was a strategically vital city on the western end of the Chalcidice, the region that included the three finger-like projections of land into the northwestern Aegean Sea. Potidaea itself spanned the isthmus that connected the mainland of the Chalcidice to its westernmost peninsula, Pallene. The port at Potidaea provided Athens a vital pipeline to resources from the Chalcidice, Macedon, and Thrace. The Athenian citizenry saw Macedon and Thrace as undependable, even barbaric, but supply needs and logistics trumped national pride, especially in a time of war.

Potidaea, like Hippocrates' home island of Kos, had been a tribute state of Athens, part of the Delian League formed decades earlier to keep Greece secure from further invasions by Persia. As the years passed, though, Athens had become heavy-handed in its demands for tribute, and the League became less a federation of allies than an Athenian empire in all but name. Members of the League had tried to rebel every so often, most notably the island states of Naxos and Thasos, but none had succeeded in overthrowing Athens as undisputed ruler of the Aegean.

The problem with Potidaea was that it was a colony of Corinth, the commercial superpower on the isthmus between Athenian territory and the Spartan-dominated Peloponnese. Corinth had fought a bloody battle against Athens and her naval ally two years earlier off the northwest coast of Greece. It was a fight that left an unsatisfactory taste in the mouths of Corinth's ruling elites. Their backing of a rebellion in Potidaea was just the thing to keep the drums of war beating.

The trireme landed on the eastern beach of the Pallene peninsula where the Athenians were camped. The oarsmen and crew worked quickly to disembark and empty the ship of arms and supplies. As something of an honored guest, Hippocrates was directed to the tent of Phormio, son of Asopius, Athenian general and commander of the operations in the Chalcidice region.

As was customary for the board of ten commanding Generals, or *strategoi,* of the Athenian army, Phormio wore a bronze helmet on his crown. Though the position of *strategos* was anything but regal, the helmet enhanced the aura of authority commanded from the rank-and-file. His features were less brutish than Kleitos', but Phormio was still not a man to be trifled with, thought Hippocrates.

Phormio rose to embrace the noted physician. "Hippocrates, it's an honor. Kleitos sent word you wished to add your skills to the siege effort."

"The honor is mine, Commander," said Hippocrates. "I'm not sure if I'd use quite those words, but yes, I'm here to hone my skills in battlefield medicine."

Phormio let out a guffaw. "I'm afraid you're a little late, Asklepiad. The battle's long since over. The troops sent by Corinth to support the uprising have been chased off, and the Potidaeans are trapped inside the city's fortifications. We've built a wall north of the isthmus and are actively building one south of the city. The fleet has blockaded the port. It's just a matter of time before the city surrenders."

"Why the reinforcements, then, if I may ask?"

"We have a fair number of injured from the battle. Our servants are decent enough at patching up wounds, but some of the men have been in agony with unset fractures and fevers of one form or another. I hope you can help them out. The reinforcements will help with the next phase of the campaign. While the Corinthians and Potidaeans engaged us on the field, small villages throughout the Chalcidice were abandoned. The inhabitants have since gathered at Olynthus, a city some seven miles from here. They're peasants and no real threat to our armies, so we'll leave them where they are. Our plan is to lay waste to these lands."

"If the peasants are no threat, why raze their homes and farms?"

Phormio's expression turned icy, and his gaze fixed on Hippocrates. "We are now at war, Asklepiad. The Athenian assembly will brook no rebellion from its tribute states, no matter how wealthy or skilled its citizens might be." Phormio paused to let the threat register. "If you don't mind tending to the injured, Asklepiad, I have plans to review with my officers."

"As you wish, Commander." Hippocrates bowed out of Phormio's quarters, where a guard escorted him to the tent of the wounded. Most of the injured were fit but out of commission with broken bones or peripheral wounds. Two of the men lay on goatskins, moaning with oozing, necrotic wounds on their flanks, deep but not mortal injuries from enemy spears. One soldier was clearly delirious, combating rigors from an amputated foot with a gangrenous stump. Slave-boys flittered around the tent, fetching bandages or jugs of water as the medic on duty ordered.

The medic noticed Hippocrates and dashed forward to bow in his presence. He was slight and young, barely past age twenty by looks. "Esteemed Asklepiad, I am graced by your presence. I am Artemisios."

"Someday people will learn to stop bowing to physicians like gods," Hippocrates murmured under his breath. "Do stand, my friend. Are you the lone physician here at the camp? Who have you trained under?"

"I'm no physician, Asklepiad," said Artemisios. "I'm an archer with the light infantry contingent. But to answer your question, yes, I am the only medic on duty here."

"How did you end up as the chief medic?"

"I'm supposed to be only an assistant. The experienced battle medic is there." Artemisios pointed at the delirious amputee.

"I see. I don't have the time and resources to educate you as I would my students, but I'll give you a brief lesson in the precepts of the medical Art. After that, we'll tend to the urgently wounded, then come back to deal with the minor injuries."

Artemisios lacked a natural talent to grasp the principles of the Art. Lamentable, thought Hippocrates, as the youth was eager to see his comrades return to health. He proved an able assistant, however, and followed Hippocrates' instructions diligently. Hippocrates laid out a plan to amputate the medic's infected leg as soon as the necessary supplies could be procured, then set about cleaning and debriding the two flank wounds.

It was after the supper meal when Hippocrates had a chance to assess the lesser injuries. He noticed a hoplite – a heavy infantryman drawn from the citizen body – tossing and turning in discomfort, trying to find a restful position with a cumbersome splint and bandage on his left arm. "What happened to your arm?"

The hoplite had a stocky physique, receding hairline, and wide, almost porcine snout. "Nothing heroic, I'm afraid. My squad was engaged in a combat drill. Someone two or three ranks behind me didn't know right from left. A cascade of bodies and shields later, and here I am."

"Who splinted the arm? It's straighter than a javelin."

"I did," said Artemisios. "I broke my arm twice when I learned to use a bow. That's how mine was bandaged each time."

Hippocrates chuckled. "And if this man was an archer, that would be fine. But his left arm doesn't hold a bow, it holds a shield."

"I don't understand," said Artemisios.

"The muscles and tendons stiffen from disuse while the fracture heals," said Hippocrates. "By the time the bone is fully fused, he'll have no use of the arm at all, or at least no ability to carry a shield. Come, let's remove the bandages and splint.

I'll walk you through how to splint an arm into its natural position."

The hoplite kept quiet while Hippocrates undressed the arm and demonstrated the proper splinting and bandage technique. It took a few tries for Artemisios to catch on, but eventually the hoplite's discomfort eased.

"You're the famous physician from Kos, are you not?" asked the hoplite.

"I can't speak to my fame, but yes, I'm a physician from Kos," said Hippocrates.

"So you're of the guild of Asklepios, then?"

"I am. Any self-described physician that hasn't sworn the Oath is a charlatan."

"Do you believe the work of a physician has value?"

Hippocrates was taken aback. "I'm sorry. You don't?"

"This sort of work, absolutely," said the hoplite. "You're restoring the injured and the sick to their normal occupation or activity. Assuming all the men here recover, we can return to the battlefield. And the same logic, I suppose, applies to a carpenter or potter incapacitated by some wound or ailment."

"And here I thought restoring the injured or the sick was what I do in a day. Please enlighten me, good hoplite. What part of a physician's work has no value...by your eyes, that is?"

"Please, Asklepiad, I mean no disrespect. I'm deeply grateful for your assistance."

"You haven't answered my question."

"You're of quicker wit than most of my interlocutors, Asklepiad, so I'll cut to the point. Have you, as a practitioner of the physician's Art, never doubted the virtue in extending good-for-nothing lives?"

"I don't recall any tutor of mine granting me the authority to judge. Please clarify what makes a life good-for-something or good-for-nothing."

"Can we agree that there are some men who are indolent, that fill themselves with waters and winds, as if the body was a marsh?"

"Of course," said Hippocrates.

"And as a consequence, spend much of their lives in a sickly condition? With nothing to do but attend upon themselves?"

"Not commonly, but yes."

"And because of their condition, they are unable to carry on a normal craft or business, nor serve in any capacity at war?"

"Necessarily so," said Hippocrates, having little choice but to agree.

"And their condition requires that the guild of Asklepios must continually name more diseases, such as flatulence? For which new remedies must be discovered and tested?"

"You've mistaken symptoms for disease, but what's your point?"

"My point is that such wretched and weak men, too sickly to be of use to the State, nevertheless demand much of a physician. And by virtue of their incurable complaints, do they not, in effect, steer the very direction of the medical Art? Away from the curable and towards the languid and unproductive?"

"So care of the chronically sick, the – as you put it – 'incurable'...you feel that practicing such medicine is without value?" Who is this ass, thought Hippocrates.

"Exactly! Why lengthen good-for-nothing lives, and enable weak fathers to beget weak sons? Except, I suppose, to enrich the physician, assuming the ill man has resources."

Hippocrates stroked his beard for a moment. "Where are you from, hoplite?"

"I'm from Alopeke, just outside the walls around Athens."

"Ever been across the great sea, to the desert kingdoms?"

"No, I have not, Asklepiad."

"Have you ever seen a man or woman with a goiter?"

"I've heard of the disorder. It's a swelling around the throat, is it not?"

"It is. Most who suffer with it have many constitutional complaints – poor appetite, sleep difficulty, tiredness, and so on. It can go on for months, even years."

"It sounds like quite an awful affliction."

"It is. And by your rationale, unworthy of a physician's effort, is that correct?"

"If the man or woman is rendered unproductive and sickly, why prolong their misery?"

"Indulge me while I share a story," said Hippocrates. "A man with a goiter was brought to my temple on Kos, a slave from the deserts beyond Egypt. The goiter had grown steadily over the months, while the master, a merchant, completed his various business affairs. Over time, the slave no longer had the strength to work many hours."

"Why not let the slave die and acquire another?"

"Along with manual labor, the slave served in the job of translator for the merchant. In the lands beyond Egypt, a skilled translator is a rare commodity, and expensive to hire for frequent but singular episodes. To the merchant, it seemed a wiser use of money to see if the slave might be cured."

"A reasonable endeavor, then."

"Within days of his stay at the temple, I had barely begun to measure his intake and output or get a sense of the timing of his symptoms. Yet without any attempts at cure on my part, his disease seemed to abate, and his energy began to improve. Within weeks he returned to full strength and the goiter was actively regressing."

"Did you feel it was coincidence? Intervention of the gods?"

"The gods neither cause nor cure disease, and coincidence would be the conclusion of a lazy intellect. No, I learned that in his native land, the typical diet contains no shellfish or salty vegetation. As I had never seen such a condition, I concluded that some reagent was either absent or superabundant in his native diet. Eating as a Greek reversed all his ailments." As would be expected when an iodine deficiency was successfully treated.

"Very impressive, Asklepiad."

"Would you agree there was merit in treating his complaints then, given that he returned to normal function?"

"I could reach no other conclusion."

"Then was I right to inquire about his condition? To seek out causes of his symptoms that might be reversed?"

"Necessarily so."

"And yet his symptoms had been present for months and months. He was chronically ill and steadily deteriorating. But had I not accepted his case, had I simply declared his life to be – using your words – 'good-for-nothing', I would never have known. Nor would anyone now know that the cure for a goiter is dietary, a finding that will henceforth be passed from physician to physician through the ages."

"I concur."

"Will you acknowledge, then, that there is a flaw with your judgement of the medical Art? That as it is impossible to know in advance who might be cured and who might not, there is merit, value, and even duty in accepting all comers into the physician's care?"

"I will certainly re-examine my opinion."

"What's your name, hoplite?"

"Socrates, son of Sophroniscus."

"A word to the wise, Socrates. Be mindful of where you run your mouth. Judging the value of another man's work without being part of his brotherhood is fraught with both hazard and error. If you're not careful, it might even get you killed."

"Understood, Asklepiad."

"Now go bother someone else. I have actual work to do."

NINE

"Medic! Medic!" The hoplite tore down one of the hides that marked the tent opening and planted his spear in the dirt. Artemisios darted upright from the hide where he'd been fast asleep and grabbed the nearest lantern. Taking direction from the hoplite, he drew open the tent completely, and stood aside as four other troops pulled in a cart carrying General Kleitos. Kleitos winced and cursed in a muffled voice but refused to cry out as the troops hoisted him from the cart by the shoulders and transferred him to Hippocrates' procedure table.

Hippocrates had been dozing off as he recorded his days' notes, but the flourish of troops and clanging of armor jolted him wide awake. "What's happened?"

Two of the soldiers gathered every nearby lantern to shine on their field commander. Kleitos had a tourniquet wrapped around the left thigh, a means to slow the bleeding from a massive gash midway between the hip socket and knee. The wound itself was packed with cloths the troops carried for bandages and slings on the battlefield. "This gods-cursed war," groaned Kleitos.

One of the soldiers spoke. "We were on the march to set up an encampment on the west end of the peninsula. We came across a family farmstead, stragglers from the peasants' exodus. We put the man of the house and his eldest son to the sword, and took the woman and younger boy as slaves. When the General walked by, one of the children lunged at him with a sickle. We've done what we can with the wound, but..."

A woman's scream from outside pierced the night. "Help! Help! My son!"

Hippocrates signaled a slave to fetch supplies and darted outside to check the commotion. A boy no older than ten lay on the ground convulsing, his eye turned down and outwards. Hippocrates took a lantern and inspected the boy's head. The skin was broken on the right temple, and the ambient light revealed a sharp indentation in the exposed bone. A blow with a hammer, thought Hippocrates, or maybe the hilt of a sword.

Bound in ropes, the woman dropped to her knees. "Please! Save him! He didn't mean to hurt the commander."

Before Hippocrates could answer, Phormio and his lieutenants marched on scene. "What's going on? Why has Kleitos' regiment come back to camp? And why is there a woman here shrieking?"

"We encountered this family while marching to the new campsite, General," said the solider holding the slaver's ropes. "The boy attacked Kleitos. We struck him as a warning. This is his mother."

"Asklepiad, how severe is the boy's injury?" said Phormio.

"Very," said Hippocrates grimly. "The outturned eye and convulsions are a grave sign."

Phormio seized his lieutenant's short sword. He cut the boy's throat, then stood and slit the mother's. "Cart the bodies back to their farmhouse and burn them inside it. Return with the livestock and any harvested food."

"You're a butcher!" shouted Hippocrates. The crowd of soldiers froze in silence a moment.

"Patch up Kleitos' wounds," said Phormio, handing the sword to a servant for cleaning. "Out of respect for your service to my men, Asklepiad, I'm willing to attribute your insubordinate cries to a lack of sleep. But you are a guest here. You'd be wise not to test the limits of my patience."

"I – thank you, Commander. Understood," said Hippocrates. He waved away the entourage of soldiers and arranged the lanterns around the procedure table to keep it as brightly lit as possible. At his direction, two slave-boys lifted a small wooden chest and placed it gently by Kleitos' neck. Hippocrates leafed through the chest's contents and produced a chunk of brittle yellow cake. He ground the cake in a mortar, then held it over a lantern flame until vapors appeared. "Kleitos, I need you to breathe this in."

"What is it?" said Kleitos.

"The Persians call it 'poppy's tears'. It'll dull the pain better than the strongest uncut wine. The Egyptians have been using it since before the pyramids were built."

"This isn't what they give those initiates at Eleusis, is it?" A day's march northwest of Athens, Eleusis was the principal worship site for the cult of Demeter and Persephone.

Hippocrates watched as Kleitos' pupils constricted in response to the vapors. "I wouldn't know. Nobody initiated into the Eleusinian cult ever speaks of it. But I've heard whispers about the visions and behaviors some are said to experience at Eleusis. The descriptions don't match anything I've seen when administering this."

Kleitos' eyes glazed over as the drug took effect. "You're not making many friends here."

Hippocrates took out a needle carved from a tapered bone and threaded a thick fiber of flax through its eye. "I'm here to work, General. If I wanted to be with friends I'd have stayed on Kos or gone to Athens."

Hippocrates set the suture aside then fished a sea sponge from a barrel of water and squeezed it out. "This won't be comfortable," he said. "I'm going to remove the tourniquet and bleed the wound into the sponge. The gash is fresh, but if the sickle was old or rusted, bleeding the wound will help prevent tetanus. After that I'll cauterize it with a hot iron and sew you up. You should be back in fighting form in a few weeks."

Kleitos took another few whiffs of poppy vapor. "Fighting? Ha! We'll be rotated out of here once the winter rains have ceased."

"Rotated out? We haven't even been here one year. They're going to rotate troops so soon?"

"We were late in getting here, Asklepiad, well after the siege was underway. The walls are built. Phormio's talents might be of use here, I suppose, if Athens decides to invade other parts of the Chalcidice. But many of his troops need a breather in Athens before redeployment or are overdue for a stint in office. One way or the other, keeping a force this large at Potidaea is expensive, and this isn't where the war will be won or lost."

Hippocrates cursed under his breath, packing Kleitos' wound with the sponge and removing the tourniquet.

"What's the matter?" said Kleitos. "You thought you'd be part of a great, glorious war? Above the fray, doing the work of the god Apollo with your bandages and herbs? A hero out of Homer in your own right?

"'A wise physician skill'd our wounds to heal,
Is more than armies to the public weal'.

"You know," said Hippocrates, "most of the people I give those vapors to go unconscious. They don't start reciting Homer." Hippocrates wrapped a cloth around his hand and picked a glowing iron rod off a brazier. Tossing away the blood-soaked sponge, he rolled the iron rod across both sides of Kleitos' gash, filling the tent with the fumes of singed flesh.

"In the name of...that's painful!" hollered Kleitos, pushing his nose deeper into the opiate smoke.

"Sorry, General," said Hippocrates. "That will be the worst of it. Stitching the wound together won't be pleasant but I sharpened the needle just today."

Kleitos pointed to a massive scar above his collarbone. "Ever been impaled by a spear that barely misses your throat? I think I can handle a needle prick.

"'While thus the hero's pious cares attend
The cure and safety of his wounded friend...'

"You must have a favorite passage, Asklepiad. If a witless warlord like me learned to read from Homer, surely an educated man such as yourself can boast the same."

"As a boy I tried to learn the *Iliad* by heart. My father told me that in the time before Athens was a democracy, even before all of Greece was ruled by tyrants, people used to listen to storytellers recite the entire *Iliad* over three days. I thought if a wandering poet could do it, why not me?" Hippocrates brushed out the wound and started suturing it closed. "What a fruitless exercise that was until an actor told me that the secret lies in the epithets. All those countless little phrases – 'shield-bearing Zeus' or what have you – are there to keep the meter and flow of the poem intact. Once you grasp that, even the longest passages are a cinch to remember. What a simple but elegant solution...but you asked for a favorite passage. I've always liked the close of Polydamas' counsel to Hector:

"'To some the powers of bloody war belong,
To some, sweet music, and the charm of song;
To few, and wondrous few, has Zeus assigned
A wise, extensive, all-considering mind.'

"Man's achievements aren't confined to the battlefield, General. For me it's the Art. It sustains me, it drives me, yet its wonders still astound me. A gift of the gods, if not their work."

"The gods have given you another gift, Asklepiad...a second chance at peace, if you'll accept it from my hands rather than theirs. I'll not be fit to hold a spear again in the field, even with your fine work. Nor do I have any interest in listening to the philosophers and demagogues of the Athenian assembly come the spring. I'm inviting you on my ship back to Kos once she's able to hoist sail and I'm able to walk without aid. You can step away from this war before all the lands of Greece lie in ruin, to practice your Art on Kos and live your life in tranquility."

Hippocrates finished suturing and wrapped a dry bandage around Kleitos' leg. "A career solider, suggesting I abandon the war?"

Kleitos grimaced as he sat up from the table, waving off assistance as the intoxicating opium fog began to fade.

"'Better from evils, well foreseen, to run,
Than perish in the danger we may shun.'

"I'm a career solider that's seen too many men fall to the spear to find nobility or purpose in battle. I came here out of duty, a duty I've now discharged. The same holds true for you, my friend."

The men embraced, and Hippocrates lent himself as a crutch for Kleitos to hobble to a sheepskin close by. "It's a tempting invitation, General, but I've more work to do in service of the Art. Whether it's here, in Athens, or elsewhere on the seas or mainland, the gods aren't willing me home just yet."

"If you say so, Asklepiad," said Kleitos, "but be careful how much trust you put in the whims of immortal gods.

"'Zeus weighs affairs of earth in dubious scales,
And the good suffers, while the bad prevails.'"

TEN

"Onesimos!" The chief rigger, a burly and illiterate Thracian, spoke a pitiful and broken Greek. Useless on land, even in a fight, the brute nevertheless had a gift with the sail that made him indispensable to the trader's crew. "One slave, he sick. Come, see! Blood!"

"What?!?" Onesimos murmured a few words to his helmsman, asking him to let the sails out for a slower approach into the Piraeus. "What do you mean, he's sick and there's blood?" Was one of the slaves hurt and bleeding, or was he struck with disease? Onesimos kept the slave-men tied loosely in the open-air cargo hold, either to one another or to heavier items of cargo. He'd been feeding them regularly to better the odds of a strong sale price, but choppy autumn waters and uncooperative winds had made the trip longer and harder than he'd hoped.

Onesimos was perennially annoyed by the prospect of walking around the boat while at sea, more so in uncalm conditions. The rigging of the mast and sail ran most of the length of the deck, and the ropes controlling the sail were under constant adjustment. The broad, square sail was mounted transverse on a yardarm at the midline of the upper mast. Mounting the sail that high helped to prevent a thick gust of wind from flinging a crewman overboard. But the mess of ropes that turned and raised the yardarm, and the longer ropes at the helm that directly adjusted the sail, were easy to trip over or tangle a limb in. A sudden gale while making one's way from stern to midship made things even more perilous, and Onesimos could name more than one seaman who'd broken his neck while stopping to admire a pile of cargo. He took his time weaving methodically between the standing rigging that stayed the mast and the lighter ropes that worked the sail.

For a man born and raised in the Aethiopian sun, the slave looked wan. His head bobbed in feverish delirium while his arms massaged a bloated belly. He had a meek staccato cough that splattered droplets of blood on his chest and naked genitals. Onesimos snapped a finger and shook the slave by the shoulders, getting only a groan in return.

What had Kenamon said about this bunch? 'You've never seen such a gods-cursed lot. Human pack-mules living among the rats, all of them. We found them sleeping in shacks with enough rat droppings lining the floor to fill a cistern. They're better off as slaves in Greece than making a king's ransom living as they do.'

The chief rigger lumbered into the hold. "I give water, he no want. I leave water, he no take, spit blood."

Onesimos leaned to get a closer look at the slave's eyes. "You! Can you hear me? Are you awake?"

The slave jerked his head back, coughing louder. He vomited a large volume of blood on himself, then fell unconscious in shock.

"Gods!" hollered Onesimos, extending an arm to his crew chief. "Hand me your knife and get some men down here!" He slashed the at slave's ropes and jogged astern to shout at the helmsman and other riggers. "Bring to! The sail...pull the ropes and raise the sail completely!" The helmsman raised a signal and the ship was brought to a standstill, drifting on the waves. The spare crewmen gathered around the languid slave for their orders.

"Throw him over the gunwale into the drink," said Onesimos. "Then find an empty water jug and use seawater to wash the floors. I can't have his rat-pissed blood tainting the foodstuffs." This gods-cursed slave trade, he thought. He stood and shouted at the rest of the slaves. "Anyone else going to try and die before we pull into port?"

Not speaking a word of Greek, the slaves shrugged their shoulders in confusion, aghast as their dying brother was thrown overboard like the carcass of an animal dead too long to be eaten.

The crew hustled to clean up the bloody mess. With the winter solstice fast approaching, there were precious few minutes of sunlight to waste any given day. While the blood was cleared from the cargo hold, Onesimos and the helmsman discussed whatever change in speed or bearing might be needed to reach port on schedule.

As the sail was unfurled and the ship resumed course, the wind and sea spray hid the groans of another slave, clearing his itchy throat and rubbing a watery eye.

ELEVEN

The grim, overcast skies and cool, steady drizzle reflected the mood of the Athenians, as each citizen marched in somber procession. This day would mark the first public funeral in nearly two generations, since heroes of the Persian wars fell in defense of their free and democratic city-state. A crowd of thousands, that would normally be scattered about the bustling social center of Athens, the *agora*, walked in silence along the Panathenaic Way, a wide processional road that bisected the city marketplace from southeast to northwest. Gorgias and Democritus were among a crowd of foreigners trailing the Athenian citizenry, their steps matching the rhythm of the dirges chanted by the black-garbed widows of fallen soldiers.

The most prominent Athenian leaders, religious and political, led the crowd, followed by the family and friends of the dead. The bones of the dead rested in cypress coffins, each coffin pulled on a large wooden cart. There were eleven carts in all, one for each of the ten Athenian tribes, with the eleventh left empty in honor of those whose remains were unrecovered from the battlefield.

The procession passed northwest out of the *agora* to Outer Kerameikos, the so-called Beautiful Suburb, an area that included the state graveyard for soldiers and citizens of the affluent classes. Outer Kerameikos lay just beyond the Dipylon, the largest gate along the northern edge of the defensive stone walls that encircled Athens and her ports.

Once the procession reached the public graveyard, the mourning family members tore out locks of hair and left them as offerings to their dead beloved. Next, they poured libations for the deceased, mixtures of wine, oils, and perfumes. A black bull was ushered to a dais with an altar, its frightened bleats the only noise not part of the funeral hymns chanted by the crowd. A leading priest sung a ritual incantation, sacrificing the animal as a blood offering. The bones of the dead were laid in their respective graves, as mourners poured a final libation and left offerings of honey, grain meal, and fruits.

When all the fallen were interred, Pericles, First Citizen of Athens, stood atop the dais for the customary public eulogy. "Most of my predecessors in this place have commended him who made this speech part of the law, telling us that it is well that it should be delivered at the burial of those who fall in battle..."

Though well in the back of the crowd, Gorgias and Democritus had no difficulty hearing the calming, resonant voice of Pericles. "So, Teacher," whispered Democritus, "how does the great man of Athens' public speaking compare with yours?"

"Do you ever stop finding excuses to harass me?" Gorgias whispered back. "It's a solemn occasion, and I'm doing my solemn best, both to maintain composure and to avoid exposure. But to answer your question, I'm an admirer of this vaunted man. His reputation for oratory is well earned. Though his diction might be without flower, his words resonate with an obvious power, teeming with moral suasion and moral authority."

"...We cultivate refinement without extravagance and knowledge without effeminacy," continued Pericles. "Wealth we employ more for use than for show, and place the real disgrace of poverty not in owning to the fact but in declining the struggle against it...we have forced every sea and land to be the highway of our daring, and everywhere, whether for evil or for good, have left imperishable monuments behind us..."

"Imperishable monuments...no kidding," whispered Democritus. "Have you spent much time up on that Acropolis?"

"Not if I can help it," said Gorgias. "The daytime sun is too punishing. Does the assembly ever stop approving building projects up there? The mammoth mountains of marble, the gilded and gaudy sculptures..."

"All for the glory of Athens," said Democritus plainly.

"You're of a different mind?" said Gorgias.

"I'm not Athenian. Even as a philosopher, the state of my mind doesn't matter."

Pericles continued, "...For this offering of their lives made in common by them all they each of them individually received the renown which never grows old, and for a sepulcher, not so much that in which their bones have been deposited, but that noblest of shrines wherein their glory is laid up to be eternally remembered upon every occasion on which deed or story shall call for its commemoration...These take as your model and, judging happiness to be the fruit of freedom and freedom of valor, never decline the dangers of war..."

"You see?" said Gorgias, "He can use the tricks of my trade in a speech, if he has need."

"Alliteration now counts as a trick?" said Democritus. "Don't let Hippocrates hear you say that. He'll boast that even his toddler knows the 'tricks' you charge wealthy families to teach to their sons."

"...but fortunate are they who draw for their lot a death so glorious as that which has caused your mourning, and to whom life has been so exactly measured as to terminate in the happiness in which it has been passed. Still I know that this is a hard saying, especially when those are in question of whom you will constantly be reminded by seeing in the homes of others blessings of which once you also boasted..."

A stranger in front of the foreigners, of slender build and roughly Democritus' age, was frantically scratching notes on a scroll. Democritus tapped on his shoulder and asked, "are you recording his words?"

"The crux of the speech, if not the text verbatim," the man whispered in response. "I've never been moved so deeply by a funeral oration. The speeches I've heard from our First Citizen are truly a gift for all time." Pericles concluded his speech, waving away the crowd to file back behind the city walls. "Were you not touched?"

"By the ceremony, absolutely," said Democritus. "I felt a pang of grief with every note of the mourners' hymns. But the speech delved too deeply into the politics of the war for my tastes, if I'm to tell the truth."

"Dark days lie ahead," said the stranger, "and Athens needs words of strength and inspiration to get through them.

The heroic dead can take comfort in eternal glory."

"While the living must make do with pain and in fear," said Democritus, extending a hand in greeting. He introduced himself and his famed Sophist teacher.

"I'm Thucydides, son of Olorus. I've heard both your names spoken of around the *agora*. Probably at a *symposium* or two as well, but wine at a party does funny things to the memory. It's my pleasure to meet you both." The men embraced in turn. "What brings you two to Athens in a time of war?"

"We are heralds of the healer Hippocrates," said Gorgias, "living reservoir of medical knowledge, to whom we pay most humble homage—"

"Do remember, Teacher, this is still a funeral," said Democritus. He turned to Thucydides. "We're laying the groundwork for our physician friend to practice his Art...finding a spot for the temple of healing, recruiting prospective students, procuring common reagents in bulk, and so forth. He should arrive shortly after the winter rains end."

"I have connections to the political leadership," said Thucydides. "Shall I arrange for him to speak before the assembly?"

"I've no doubt he'll be honored, but he should decide for himself," said Democritus. "We'll make sure you're introduced soon after he arrives."

"A pleasure to meet you both," said Thucydides, bowing away and back towards the Dipylon Gate.

"Come, let's find shelter," said Gorgias. "Those clouds from the southeast appear even more ominous than the ones overhead."

"Let's pray those clouds carry only the rain, Teacher," said Democritus. "I've had enough gloom and metaphor today to last a generation."

TWELVE

Hippocrates took deep, refreshing breaths of a crisp spring breeze blowing across the foredeck as the flotilla of triremes sped across the Bay of Phalerum southwest of Athens. Unlike the ragtag band of islanders that Hippocrates hitched a to Potidaea with, the crews under Phormio's command belonged to a trained, professional navy. Even in the tight quarters of a narrow warship, few of the oarsmen worked up a sweat propelling a trireme any slower than six knots.

The town of Phalerum, on the eastern edge of the bay, had been the principal port of Athens and Attica a century earlier. But war with the Persians changed the defensive strategy of the Athenians. Themistocles, the naval commander who led the Athenian fleet to victory at Salamis a half-century earlier, had pressed for the more defensible harbor at Piraeus to supplant Phalerum as Athens' main port. Phalerum still saw a smattering of naval activity, and it was a useful place for sailors to come ashore if sailing conditions changed rapidly, but the commercial shipyards had long since made the permanent move.

The six-mile wall between Athens and Phalerum formed the eastern boundary of a wedge-shaped territory sheltering Athens from rest of the Greek mainland, with the northern Long Wall to Piraeus forming a northwestern boundary. The walls had left Athens potentially vulnerable to an amphibious attack from the bay, though no enemy had dared to oppose Athens' navy in the region since the Persians. Once the middle Long Wall was built between Athens and Piraeus, the capital was effectively walled off from invasion.

Hippocrates had largely kept to his work through the winter. The siege at Potidaea entered a period of stalemate. The city's inhabitants were secure enough in their provisions to put off surrender, but behind defensive walls that precluded a direct Athenian assault. As Kleitos had predicted, winter's end meant a rotation of troops. Tempted as he was to take up Kleitos' offer of a return trip to Kos, Hippocrates opted to follow through on his plan to serve the war effort. Having spent most of the winter avoiding further head-butting with

Phormio, he hitched a ride with the squadron of triremes returning to Athens.

Hippocrates held a tight grip on the bulwark, gingerly making his way along the deck to the ship's aft. "Captain," he shouted above the din of the sea spray, "I congratulate you on the performance of your oarsmen. My voyage to Potidaea was nowhere as smooth." The captain shrugged and nodded in response, concerned more with a flag signal from another trireme on portside. "The trip will be over soon enough, I suppose," Hippocrates murmured too softly to be heard.

The Piraeus dominated the peninsula due west-southwest from Athens. There were three functioning ports at Piraeus, all protected by guarded extensions of the parallel Long Walls. The smaller harbors served strictly as ports for the navy. The massive Grand Harbor, with ready access to both Piraeus' *agora* and the Long Wall corridor, was the primary site for commercial activity and shipbuilding.

As the triremes docked one by one, Hippocrates gaped at Piraeus with the awe of a child. Hundreds, if not thousands of soldiers, dockworkers, shipbuilders, masons, all marching, hoisting, hammering away – toiling – in the late morning sun, in dozens of ship-houses, warehouses, checkpoints, and half-built administrative buildings...

...and off in the distance, a brisk day's walk northeast, the gleaming Acropolis of Athens.

A random nudge snapped Hippocrates out of his fanciful gazing, as crewmen extended a gangplank onto the dock for the contingent of hoplites aboard to disembark. A clamor of armor plates and helmets smacking and clanging soon followed, as troops left the boat and fell into formation where dry land met the pier. Hippocrates found a crewman he'd been friendly with through the winter and slipped the man a few drachmae to help bring his medical supplies safely ashore. He spent a few more minutes surveying the bustle of the port, then plotted a path to the barracks he's spend a night or two in before making his way to Athens.

As he instructed the barrack slaves around the handling of his belonging, he heard a howl from the watchtower a few yards away. "Help! Medic! Medic! Anyone! I'm injured and can't get up!"

Hippocrates darted to the tower and up the stairs, discovering a youth in light armor, sitting propped up against a parapet, nursing a bandaged cut on his leg. "I'm Hippocrates, son of Heraclides, Physician of Kos. What's happened to you?"

"Well met, Physician. I've heard of your legendary reputation. I'm Aristophanes, son of Philippus."

"Legendary, you say?" said Hippocrates with a snicker. "I think you're mistaking me for my ancestors."

"Oh no, Sir," said Aristophanes, "every great man of Athens, every military leader, they all say the same thing: if you have need of a physician, you must seek the services of Hippocrates, son of Heracles."

"Heraclides," laughed Hippocrates. "Heracles killed the Hydra and captured a giant three-headed dog. My father owned orchards and taught medicine."

"Deepest apologies, most honored Physician. I would never endeavor to dishonor your family."

"Never endeavor...everyone's a poet. How did you get that cut you've bandaged up?"

"I fell on my spear."

Hippocrates chuckled. "Don't you mean fell on your sword? If so, you've survived the ordeal remarkably intact. When Ajax tried it at the siege of Troy, he ended up dead."

"No allusions to legend, honored Physician. It was the spear that caused this injury."

"How? That spear is five cubits long end-to-end. You're what, three-and-a-half cubits tall, four on your tiptoes? How can you fall on a spear that's taller than you?"

"It's rather embarrassing, but I was removing a pebble from my sandal and tripped while the tip sat atop a brick. It scraped my leg and I went down hard."

Went down hard? Apart from the bandage, the young man seemed the picture of health, thought Hippocrates. "Let's see this injury." Aristophanes stripped off his dressings, revealing a superficial scrape most men would scarcely notice.

"Young man, there's barely a spot of blood here."

"Oh, but the fall. The throbbing ache in the leg is so awful. I'm struggling to stay upright," said Aristophanes, grimacing as his knee buckled over and over while standing up. "I don't think I can stay on patrol this week."

Hippocrates stared blankly.

"Could I make a request of you?" said Aristophanes. "Would you be willing to craft a letter – either on a scroll or a tablet – stipulating that I should be off patrol duty until the leg heals?"

"I'm sorry...you want a physician's note to get you out of military service?" said Hippocrates, incredulous. "That's your request?"

"No commander would ever question the word of a physician!"

"It will be a pitiful day indeed when those that practice the Art have their hours consumed by people seeking a letter to get out of duty."

"So...no note, then?"

Hippocrates lay a hand on the shoulder of the young guard. "You're afraid."

Aristophanes stood upright and went pale. "Is it that obvious?"

"It's normal. The only soldiers that charge into battle without fear are abject fools and barbarian berserkers. But take heart. There's no higher honor than dying in the defense of your city."

"Hah! You mean Athens and her assembly of assholes?"

"Son, your assembly is the envy of countless cities and towns in the mainland and colonies. And your leader Pericles is the most revered man in the Greek world."

"Pericles Almighty isn't the problem. It's the blowhards and buffoons around him that will make dog meat of us all by this war. They're drunkards, dickheads the lot of them...whore-mongrel war-mongers." Aristophanes sighed. "Tell me, Physician, is it too much to want a few more years of youthful debauchery before taking a spear in the throat?"

Hippocrates' chuckling soon became a boisterous laugh. "You have a point, Aristophanes, son of Philippus. Now tell me, if nothing else to get your mind off your fears...what's your career plan once the fighting has stopped?"

"My father's a wealthy man and provided me the luxury of an education in literature and poetry. I hope to be a playwright someday. I see myself entering the annual tragedy competitions at the festivals."

"Young man, leave tragedy to the tragedians. You, I'm quite certain, have an obvious gift for comedy."

Aristophanes bowed. "Thank you, good Physician."

"And I'll make you a deal. Take my things to the barracks and I'll write you a note good for one day's worth of debauchery. Buy yourself a jug of wine and get yourself laid if you must. But stay out of trouble and be back on patrol before sunup, or I'll have the drill instructor personally flog you for malingering."

THIRTEEN

It had felt like an age since Hippocrates had last been through the towering Piraean Gate that marked the entry into Athens proper. He was dog-tired from the four-mile trek along the defensive walls joining Athens to her main harbor. Part of his fatigue was simply the walk in the absence of any rejuvenating breeze, and part was the lingering effects of a lousy night's sleep from nervous excitement.

He had only the faintest memories of his first journey to Athens, as a child travelling alongside his father to the Panathenaea festival that year. These were the early days of Athens' transition from thriving democracy to full-borne maritime empire, even before construction began on the awesome and imposing new Parthenon. Hippocrates recalled with a boyish grin how, as he and his father walked past any important significant landmark or shrine, his father would relate one story after another about Theseus, the legendary king that brought Athens to glory in the Age of Heroes. Many of the stories Hippocrates now looked back on as folk tales – Procrustes and his iron beds of torture, the Minotaur of Crete – stories to delight or scare children, with or without a moral.

But Minotaur or no Minotaur, the legends portrayed Theseus as a capable and formidable king, and founding father to the dominant civilization of the Greek world. In those ancient days, Attica, the provincial region surrounding Athens herself, was a mosaic of independent but weak states, the landscape dotted with olive orchards and peasant farms. Theseus united those disparate communities under a single kingdom, administered from his seat of power in Athens. The kingdom of Athens protected Attica from more powerful Greek monarchies and marauding barbarian tribes.

Athens had endured for centuries after the Age of Heroes came to an end, through kings and tyrants, the birth of the democracy, and the sack by Persian invaders. But she was now an indomitable naval empire. The symbol of that imperial might was the grandeur of the Acropolis, that collection of cult temples atop the mesa in the middle of the city. Hippocrates couldn't help but look up at the Acropolis, the Parthenon in particular, with simultaneous wonder and fear.

A slap on the back broke his giddy trance. "Asklepiad," shouted Democritus, "don't stare too long. The Acropolis is as hypnotic as Homer's lotus flowers. You'll never want to leave Athens!"

Hippocrates embraced his friend in joy. "How did you know I'd be arriving today?"

"The heart of the city's not big, especially once the markets and offices of the *agora* empty out for the midday meal at the end of the workday. So I've forced myself to put off my meal each day, and brave the sun to see if you've arrived."

Hippocrates patted his close friend's ample belly. "I presume this isn't something you did each day through the winter?"

"Gods, no. Only once the naval crews started filing in from the port. I received word that the fleet from Potidaea had come into port a few days ago. I figured you'd linger in the Piraeus and lag behind the troops a couple of days, maybe two weeks at most."

"How are the accommodations?"

"Gorgias knows how to pick his students. This Polus – another teacher of rhetoric– lives in a good-sized home right around the corner from both the *agora* and Temple of Hephaestus. Not as grand as your estate, but impressive considering how densely the houses are packed into this city."

"Wait...is Gorgias' student another sophist?"

"Don't know if it pays as much as a physician's work, but rhetoric seems much more lucrative than itinerant philosophy. Polus can't attract students the way Gorgias can, but the man makes a fortune writing speeches for lawsuits. For one case that went before the popular jury, he wrote speeches for both the plaintiff and the defendant!"

"Do I even want to know how verbose he and Gorgias get come supper time?"

"No idea," said Democritus with a wink, "I guzzle my wine before taking so much as a morsel of food. I don't sober up until the two of them are barely conscious and done with their evening rambling. Then I make sure Euthalia earns her keep and it's off to bed from there."

"And to think I used to wonder why you need to pay for companionship," said Hippocrates, and the two men strolled on into Athens.

Athenian homes stood in stark contrast to the marble-rich opulence of temples and public buildings. As the city had been built and sacked and rebuilt through the centuries, houses in Athens remained shoddy in their construction, even in the wealthier neighborhoods. Not much more than stone and mud for the exterior, and slathered-on plaster for the interior, size was about the only way to tell a potter's house from his patron's.

The impossible gap in splendor between the public and private spheres of life made one thing clear: life in Athens, for the men at least, was inescapably and unapologetically social. Even the most staid and stoic family man spent his days in the *agora*, the enormous market and open forum enclosed by offices of the state. It was in the *agora* that the male citizens of Athens conducted business, peddled gossip, watched competitions in both arts and sports, and debated the political drama of the day. At this point in the afternoon the *agora* was all but empty, only a smattering of craftsmen and public officials finishing up from the workday. Tomorrow, thought Hippocrates, tomorrow I'll see it in its glory.

The house of Polus, the rhetorician-speechwriter, was nondescript from the outside and indistinguishable from its neighbors. It was closed to the outside world, but for small window holes to protect the indoors from wintertime rains. Tucked at the far end of narrow and winding alleyway, only an inscription beside the solid wood door denoted its owner.

Inside, though, was a different story. The altars to Zeus in his both household forms – protector of treasures and boundaries, respectively – and the statue of Apollo by the entry door were of rare quality and ornately adorned. As Democritus explained, "I told you he was rich. That sculpture of Apollo was made by a top apprentice of Phidias, that friend of Pericles who carved the Athena in the Parthenon and Zeus at Olympia." The courtyard and andron were similar in size to the ones Hippocrates enjoyed in his own home, and the long inside walls were painted with frescoes depicting athletic events from the Olympiad.

The friends found a pair of straw-covered couches in the andron and lay back to chat. "I'm not sure where Gorgias and Polus got to," said Democritus. "They've been known to find an audience, even on the stickiest days in Greece. We'll see them come meal time, I'm sure of it."

"How's the girl been since your arrival?" said Hippocrates.

"Thaïs? We've kept her busy with this and that. Busy and safe, just as we promised."

"And a suitable temple?"

"There's an old temple to Apollo in the northeastern neighborhood, near the gates that lead to Marathon. It's fallen into disuse since the Acropolis was built up. I spoke with the city's magistrate Euthydemus, and Gorgias pleaded your case to the King Archon. Both are 'thrilled with your commitment to serve the empire in a time of war'."

"You don't seem invested in the war effort," said Hippocrates.

"I don't need to be, Asklepiad. I'm not Athenian. But you know me. I'm a philosopher, a lover, a scholar. My passion lies in learning, and my favorite learning lies in the passions. War is too harsh a teacher for my tastes."

"I've never seen you like this, Democritus."

"Seen me how?"

"Unhappy. Bereft of cheer. Maybe even scared?"

"Maybe. Haven't thought about it, to be honest."

"So what have you been thinking? Surely a philosopher spends a good deal of his days and nights doing that."

Democritus paused a moment, stroking his beard in silence. "Gorgias and I attended the state funeral right before the worst days of winter. It was magnificent, solemn, cathartic...everything you'd want or expect in the day. But it had me thinking about all the wars I've read or learned about. Troy was about *timê* and *kleos* – honor and glory – and the love of a beautiful woman."

"The face that launched a thousand ships..."

"The Persians were invaders. Our fathers and grandfathers fought to preserve our life and freedom as Greeks. Inevitable as it might seem to the politicians, this war doesn't have a greater purpose, a greater wisdom at play."

"Haven't Athens and Sparta been fighting skirmishes and proxy wars forever? My father used to tell me the news, late as it was in reaching Kos. There was the *helot* revolt in Sparta, the spat over Megara, the naval battle two years ago at Korkyra...this might not turn out as everyone fears."

"Not this time, Asklepiad. I get the sense that this is the big one, so to speak. There's a grim resolve the citizens wear on their faces. It's cast a pall on the city. There's engagement but not trust between the people...it's hard to put into words."

"You mean there's something beyond the random interplay of 'atoms'?" Hippocrates smirked.

"You're a gods-cursed shit sometimes," said Democritus with a snort. "We're guests of Athens, and I'll pay whatever tax or tribute I must. But I have an uneasy sense that slaughtering Spartans – slaughtering fellow Greeks – and making slaves of their women and children doesn't serve anything but the most bestial instincts of man. It might have been a mistake to join you here, old friend."

"The Athenian leaders, especially this Pericles, seem to know what they're doing. Besides, you're not here to fight. You're here to loiter about the *agora* and get drunk each night. I'm the one that's come to work. You're free to enjoy the safety of Athens' walls and the warmth of her hospitality.

"Put it out of your head. Revel in what the School of Greece has on offer. Or make yourself useful and join me at the temple. Or spend your days and nights – how did you put it – making Euthalia 'earn her keep'. You gain nothing from ruminating on what's beyond your control. It causes the pulse to race and the insides to purge. What may come of war is the will of the gods."

"You of all people, laying events at the feet of the gods? You and your father and your students have been sailing the seas around Greece for years now, trying to prove that the gods serve no role in the spread of disease. Tell me, Asklepiad…if the gods play no part in a plague, what makes you think they have anything to do with a war?"

FOURTEEN

Democritus pulled the wide-brimmed hat down across his eyes. "It's too early."

Hippocrates gave his old friend a slap on the back as they took a seat on the long stone bench. "Did you know that centuries ago, Greeks everywhere would gather at the crack of dawn for three straight days, just to listen to one bard reciting Homer's *Iliad*? And here you are, in the heart of Athens, about to take in a live drama, complaining about the time!"

"This entire theatre is rocking like a boat at sea," said Democritus.

"You're sitting on a stone slab set upon a minor mountain," said Gorgias. "The only thing rocking is the amphora of wine still sloshing betwixt your gullet and gut."

"It's a festival," said Democritus. "Weren't you the ones that told me I needed to relax and indulge in all that Athens had to offer? Now you begrudge me heeding your advice."

"Even during the City Dionysia, moderation reigns supreme in Athens," said Thucydides. He introduced himself to Hippocrates, and Gorgias repeated the story of their first meeting at the state funeral.

The City Dionysia was Athens' second most important religious festival, held just after the vernal equinox in honor of the god Dionysus. What was once a countryside folk festival to celebrate vineyards, the Dionysia had evolved over the centuries into five days of music, drama, and drunken hedonism. As non-Athenians, Hippocrates and his friends stood on the sidelines for most of the first day, watching the procession of revelers carry *phalloi* – oversized erect penises of wood and bronze – through the streets and into the Theatre from a distance.

The main attraction of the Dionysia, apart from the cult rituals and revelry, was the annual competition of the playwrights at the Theatre of Dionysus. Athens' most renowned dramatists entered four plays each, with the panel of judges chosen by lot. The first three plays from each dramatist, all tragedies, were often a single, connected story. The fourth play was semi-comical, a release from the emotional turmoil of watching three tragedies back-to-back.

Under perpetual construction, the Theatre took up the southeastern slope of the Acropolis mount. Anywhere from ten to more than fifteen thousand Athenians, guests, and foreign emissaries could find a seat on the stone or wood benches, arranged in tiered semi-circles for a view of the stage floor.

"Ever been to one of these performances, Hippocrates?" said Thucydides. "I know that some of the better plays have been performed elsewhere in Greece."

"Never," said Hippocrates, as excited as a child, "and I've only read snippets of scripts. As a boy, I remember seeing a collection of masks used in a performance of a work by Aeschylus. Creepy things to look at, with the hollowed eye sockets and exaggerated mouths staring back at you. I didn't sleep properly for days."

"Whose works are we to see today?" said Gorgias.

"This is another trilogy by Euripides," said Thucydides. "He lost the competition last year, placing third for his take on the revenge of Medea. It was a provocative work, though. The woman murdered her own children and flew off in the chariot of a god, but I daresay the playwright portrayed her as sympathetic. I don't think a stodgy Athenian audience was ready for it."

An Athenian noble, bedecked in garish clothing and jewelry, walked out on the circular stage floor and drew the attention of the crowd. It was the sponsor of the day's performance. "A trilogy by Euripides! The first instalment will be *Heracleidae*, the Children of Heracles."

An actor in the mask of an old man emerged from the *skene*, a small building at the rear of the stage, and stood at the prop of an altar. This was Ioalus, nephew of Heracles, whose monologue opened the production:

"This has long since been my established opinion,
The just man is born for his neighbors;"

A noble ideal, thought Hippocrates, as he watched the performance in rapt attention. It was ancient lore: the tale of Iolaus and the children of Heracles pursued by Eurystheus, Heracles' tormentor, and seeking asylum in Athens. Though he'd heard the story countless times since childhood, it was the performance – the costumes, the poetry, the songs of the chorus to drumbeats – that kept a stranglehold on Hippocrates' focus.

It was the emotional climax of the drama that took the physician's breath away, as Macaria, Heracles' daughter, justifies her own sacrifice to fulfill the prophecy of an oracle:

"...if these die, and I myself am saved,
Have I any hope to fare well;

For before now many have in this way betrayed their friends.

For who would choose to have me,

A solitary damsel, for his wife, or to raise children from me?

Therefore it is better to die than to have such an unworthy fate as this;"

At the conclusion of the play, Hippocrates stood to applaud, spellbound and in tears. Surprised at the relative lack of enthusiasm among in the crowd, he turned to Thucydides. "What's going on? Was I not supposed to do that?"

"Clearly it's your first live tragedy," said Thucydides, "and first experience with what the philosophers and dramatists call a 'purging' of the soul."

"That's an unfortunate word, considering what it means in my line of work," said Hippocrates. "But that performance was magnificent!"

"It was okay," said Thucydides with a shrug. "Last year's *Medea* was better."

"It's still too early," groaned a rising Democritus.

"Where are you off to?" said Gorgias.

"As delightful as this is, Teacher," said Democritus, "I need a piss and a bed. If I can make it to the third drama I'll see you then. If not, I'll see you come suppertime."

"I'll join you," said Hippocrates.

"You're not staying either?" said Gorgias.

"I'd love to," said Hippocrates, "but duty calls. There's a child being brought to the temple shortly, the parents quite frantic."

Hippocrates and Democritus sauntered back towards Polus' house, Democritus staggering a good deal of the way.

"I don't understand," said Hippocrates. "You came to the Theatre hung over. How is it you're barely able to stand?"

"Who says I'm hung over?" said Democritus. "I was out drinking until well into the night. In fact, I'm still feeling the wine come on now." He giggled. "Just too short on sleep to focus on death and the ire of the gods and all that. Besides, what's more in the spirit of celebrating Dionysus? Shedding a tear over poems about legends, or tossing back a jug of wine, gorging yourself on roasted ox straight from the sacrifice, and making love to a beautiful woman?"

"So it's not just Euthalia 'earning her keep'? You're sounding more and more like a true romantic with each passing day."

"Don't get me wrong, I love the girl! But it's the wine talking," said a cackling Democritus, tripping over himself and singing out of tune the rest of the way.

When they entered Polus' house, the men were taken aback by the boisterous laughter of women. There in the courtyard, Euthalia was instructing Thaïs in the flow and rhythm of veil dancing. Adorned in a gown fit for the taller and curvier Euthalia, the servant-girl spun about clumsily, hapless at every twist of the veil, in hysterics all the same.

"I told you we were keeping her busy, Asklepiad!" said Democritus. He wrapped an arm around his *hetaera* and gave her rear end a squeeze.

Thaïs dropped the veil to the ground and blushed. "I'm sorry, Asklepiad. I haven't been neglecting my chores, I just…"

"Come, now, it's festival time!" said Hippocrates. "All work and no play—"

"Makes you a physician!" said Euthalia.

"Now, Thaïs, before you wear Euthalia's dress again," said Hippocrates, "you should at least demand to know where it's been. Her clothes fall to the ground faster than an oiled wrestler on marble." The consort's familiar sneer signaled an abrupt end to the day's banter. "Take a minute to change, Thaïs, then you'll join me at the temple for a consultation."

While a growing cadre of eager young Athenians had signed up as Hippocrates' students, it was Thaïs who had quietly become the physician's preferred assistant. Unerringly polite and attentive, the girl did everything asked of her, without Hippocrates ever having to nag or repeat himself. And sure enough, while he organized his workspace at the temple,

Thaïs escorted the family of four from the temple vestibule to Hippocrates' consultation area.

The patriarch was a lean winemaker, at least a decade Hippocrates' senior. His wife, somewhere in her early twenties, nodded in silence at the exchange of greetings, nursing an infant girl in her arms. "I'm Cinesias, and this is my boy Amynias. They say you're the best Physician in all of Greece."

"Whoever 'they' are, they say a lot of things," said Hippocrates. "What's the problem with your boy?"

"The sacred disease," said Cinesias.

"You mean he gets fits, or seizures."

"The healers only ever called it the sacred disease, a pollution of the body by the gods."

"Describe the fits that he experiences."

"It starts in his arms, jerking only once. Then he lies on the ground and his entire body will go stiff and shake uncontrollably. Sometimes the fits last a second, other times they've gone far longer. It's when he turns blue and foams at the mouth that's been the most frightening. The healers claim that's a pollution by Ares. But none of their preparations or purification rituals have worked."

Hippocrates examined the boy head to toe as he spoke. "These are no healers but charlatans. How can Amynias, or any woman, child, or man for that matter, be so affected by a god? A pollution of the most impure by the most holy? And the different phases of the disease, each ascribed to a different god: if the boy speaks sharply in a seizure, Poseidon is the cause; if he loses control of his bowels, Hecate; and if he foams at the mouth, Ares. And what to make of the episodes that differ from one to the next? Are the gods so fickle as to punish a child so, toying with his life one instant to the next? There is nothing sacred to the disease, nor any other disease for that matter. The very assertion is an insult.

"And these supposed healers, who willingly take the fruits of your labor without ever providing evidence of their work? Their rituals work because Amynias went this number of days without episode? What about all the days he went without incident before coming under their care? Or those in distant lands that can't afford the voyage, yet only suffer with fits from time to time? Or barbarians with the condition, that worship alien gods outside our pantheon?

"Amynias suffers with a condition of the brain, that organ that reigns supreme in the body of a man. The disease is neither sacred nor impure, but an imbalance of natural humors and forces."

"He's our boy," said Cinesias. "Can you not cure him?"

"I can't," said Hippocrates, "but I will demonstrate how you might keep your son safe during his fits, to prevent injury. Many who have the disorder as children outgrow the condition, or at least find themselves going longer between incidents."

"Thank you, Asklepiad," said Cinesias, hugging his family in close.

"It's my duty to the Art. Disease has always been, and shall always be, a function of nature. Nature commands respect and even awe. But no natural process, even a disease, is worthy of god-given fear."

FIFTEEN

In the dusty, sun-scorched landscape of the Lavrion mines, Onesimos strained to reason with his irate associate.

"How much did I pay you?" hollered Diokles.

"Diokles, I know—" said Onesimos.

"How much did I pay you?!?"

"Fifty drachmae a head."

"You wouldn't shut up about it. 'It's ten drachmae less than the going rate', you told me, and I wouldn't need to send them back."

"I can make good on this," Onesimos pleaded. "Will you let me get a gods-cursed word in?"

The mines of Lavrion were forty miles southeast of Athens. While silver and less precious metals had been mined on and off since before the Heroic Age, it wasn't until recently that extraction of silver began in earnest. The discovery of a large vein of silver-bearing ore begat an explosion in mining at the urging of Themistocles. The mass extraction yielded hundreds of tons' worth of silver once processed. Once minted into coins, that silver financed Athens' fleet for the war against Persia, and as a consequence paved Athens' road to empire.

While the site was formally the property of the state, individual mine shafts, or even singular galleries within larger mines, could be leased by private interests in exchange for a fixed proportion of the yield going to Athenian coffers. Diokles had read the political winds before open war broke out and was three years into an expensive seven-year lease on three contiguous galleries of the southernmost mine. What he lacked in access to mine shafts, Diokles made up for by owning and managing most of the site's southernmost washeries, where low-yield grains of ore were separated and concentrated before smelting.

"Talk," said Diokles.

"How many have you lost?" said Onesimos.

"Five in the shafts just this week, plus the dozen that are listless and moaning all the gods-cursed day. I feed them, they shit it out, and can't do more than an hour's work between the lot of them. Washing ore for other lessees is the only thing keeping my operation afloat."

The Greek mines ran almost entirely on slave labor. Slaves wielded the chisels and shovels to carve the new pits and horizontal mine galleries. Slaves climbed inside the galleries to locate the ore deposits. Slaves hammered out the rock and lugged it in sacks of tanned hide. Slaves pushed the millstones that crushed rock into raw grains of ore. Slaves dumped the cisterns of rainwater into the washery sluice. Slaves scraped the washery troughs for concentrated ore. And slaves worked the smelting furnaces day and night, piling the wood that fed the fires and pumping the bellows that maintained them.

Somewhere between twenty and thirty thousand slaves worked at Lavrion, depending on the season and any discovery of a new veinlet, but the mines were a deathtrap. Countless slaves perished in the dim, stifling conditions of the pits. Others fell off a rope ladder too loosely nailed in a mine shaft. And many more choked on the toxic heat of the smelting furnaces. Lavrion was the ultimate seller's market for an enterprising slave dealer.

"The five that died...how?" said Onesimos.

"Two fell – it was from weakness, the ladders were sturdy – and the other three were found dead in a pit at the change of shift," said Diokles.

Onesimos thought a moment. "The 'moaners', as you called them. Any of them spitting or shitting blood?"

"Two, possibly a third. The one covered in boils I sent away from camp until he heals. The rest look as though they'll survive, if not recover their worth. Now I've answered your questions. What are you going to do to make this right?"

Should have burned every one of those rat-sleepers to the bone, they'll be the ruin of me, thought Onesimos. "You got a season of profitable labor out of the three you found dead. I'll refund half your money on them and split the difference with you on the injuries. As for the ones cursed by Apollo, kill the two that are purging themselves of blood. Do the same to the one with the boils that you've hidden away. Throw the bodies in a furnace and pray that will placate the ire of the gods."

"You'll refund my money on the rest?"

"No, but I'll credit you half for the three that need to be killed. If, as you say, the other nine look like they'll survive, I'll take them with me to Piraeus and have a physician restore them to strength. Kushah! Hey, Kushah!" Onesimos hailed his personal servant, who stood under an outcropping trying to find shade.

Tuta, the slave said to himself. His birth name was Tuta. It had been barely a year since he had a name and a home and a patch of land and a wife and a son. Barely a year since the men in sandals arrived in the night, butchered the elders, and gave him a choice: give in to a life of slavery, or watch his family be slaughtered at once. Barely a year since he held out his arms in surrender, only to see the men in sandals erupt in laughter, ravage his wife and murder his son.

Tuta accepted his lot but held true to his faith. As he was passed from master to master, from the man in the tunic to the man in the boat, he was given the name *Kushah*, the label for a lowly bastard of his native lands. It broke his freeborn identity but not his spirit. Tuta prayed to the gods night and day. It was not prayer for salvation – his faith would guide him to the afterlife – but rather for revenge.

His prayers would be answered swiftly, as the will of the gods dictated. Mere weeks after Tuta's capture, the man in the tunic produced a map, demanding to know where more villagers of Kush might be found. It was at that instant, when Tuta feared what countrymen he might condemn to slavery, that the hand of Set, god of violence and disorder, guided Tuta's finger, and pointed to the Despot King's work camps, the Village of the Forsaken. Now the wicked would join the wretched, suffering the wrath of Set.

"Kushah!" yelled Onesimos. "What is he, deaf?" he murmured to Diokles.

The slave felt the blistering heat take his breath away as he dashed to his unforgiving master. Illiterate even in his own language, he'd picked up enough Greek to speak a basic pidgin. "Yes. I come. Sun hot. Need dark, make no hot."

"Fine, fine, not care," said Onesimos. He pointed at a nearby cistern. "See water? Take water to sick men. Give drink. Then help up, walk to boat." The slave nodded and fetched a pail and ladle to tend to the ailing mine workers. Onesimos and Diokles continued to haggle over drachmae to be credited or refunded.

As the ladle of water passed from man to man, then man to pail, then pail to cistern, nobody noticed the wet ladle grow discolored, its surface tainted by droplets of blood from inflamed oral glands and ulcerating gums.

SIXTEEN

What madman came up with this city's model of government, Hippocrates asked himself, watching blithely as the *agora* filled in with traders and craftsmen setting up their wares. He'd been waiting outside the Tholos, the round building in the southwest *agora*, for the better part of a half-hour, while the *prytaneis*, the fifty acting executives of the democracy, finished their breakfast and daily preening.

"Surely one of them will need to come out any minute now," Hippocrates murmured under his breath, "or somebody will have to explain how anything in this city gets done."

Polus had done his best to explain the government of Athens, but even without a drop of wine on board it was hard to keep the broad details straight. Power purportedly lay with the citizen's assembly, that famed Athenian democracy, that met every ten days or more often if circumstances dictated. Even military leadership and strategy was voted on by the assembly, though it was the *strategoi* – the chief generals voted into office annually – that were responsible for planning and debating said strategy to sway the citizens' vote.

The day-to-day management of Athens, including setting the agenda for the assembly, was in the hands of the *boule*. The *boule* was a council of five hundred citizens, fifty men from each of the city's ten tribes. Each tribe rotated once through the boule in a year, with all fifty men serving as the magistrates or *prytaneis* for a forty-day month. Though the minutiae of policy were at risk of being bungled with the constant rotation of office-holders, the Athenians prided themselves on keeping extensive records of everything.

"It's as straightforward as the Gordian knot," Polus had said with a shrug. "Trying to figure it all out is probably what drives the men of Athens to drink."

The door to the Tholos finally opened and a weary-eyed man somewhere in his fifties stepped into the sunlight. The *prytaneis* were on call night and day while serving out their month of executive service. In a time of war, that entailed more than a few urgent, late-night meetings with the *strategoi*, lesser generals, and other leading Athenian citizens.

"Yes?" said the official.

"Good morning, my lord *prytanis*. I'm Hippocrates, son of Heraclides, Physician of Kos. I've come to inquire about speaking before the assembly. I believe my friend and associate, Democritus of Abdera, spoke with your counterparts some weeks ago about my pending arrival, and granting me time to speak before the citizens."

"Are you looking to speak on a matter of urgency, pertaining either to a death by homicide or to the security of the *polis*?" The official spoke with an unwavering volume and tone.

"Not at all," said Hippocrates.

"Are you an ambassador from a tribute-paying *polis*, here to discuss matters of state? Or are you here on invitation from the King Archon, here to discuss a forthcoming festival or other matter of faith?"

"No, neither of those, I don't believe." How many Archons had Polus mentioned? There was the King Archon, the Eponymous Archon...

"Very well. Come to the Bouleuterion next door during the hour at which business normally ends to speak with the official in charge of the next agenda."

"I've already been waiting here since before sunrise. Can you not just pass my name on to whoever sets the agenda?"

"Please read the procedural inscriptions outside the Bouleuterion. None save the *strategoi* or a member of the

Areopagus may apply to circumvent the conventional working hours of the *boule*."

A member of the what? Another gods-cursed thing to ask Polus about, Hippocrates moaned in his own head. "Look, I can come back to pay any fees another day, but my time is as valuable as yours. It would seem a rather minor request that my name be given to the magistrate in charge of the agenda at your convenience."

The official raised his voice but remained monotonous. "None save the *strategoi* or a member of the Areopagus may apply to circumvent the conventional working hours of the *boule*."

"Okay, okay, I understand. Can I ask what documentation I might need?"

"Please read the procedural inscriptions outside the Bouleuterion for answers to questions around documentary requirements for non-Athenian application to speak before the citizen's assembly. Should the inscriptions not answer your question, please direct your inquiry to any junior *prytanis* during conventional working hours of the *boule*."

"Do all Athenian politicians talk like this?"

"While serving as *prytaneis*, members of the *boule* are considered administrative members of the Athenian government, rather than partisan political actors. The role of *prytanis* mandates the use of language free from political inference or influence. With apologies, I now must return to my morning's duties." Without another word, the magistrate shut the door in Hippocrates' face.

"And to think I haven't even asked for any silver yet," Hippocrates said to the closed door.

There were no seriously ill Athenians at his repurposed temple in the northeast corner of the city, just a few skin lesions to excise and minor complaints to assess. Rather than dive into work that could wait until his business was done with the *boule*, Hippocrates opted to spend a few hours strolling about the *agora*, taking it all in. Even before the public offices opened, craftsmen and merchants began barking offers in the general direction of the crowd. At the massive South Stoa, the portico of unadorned columns comprising the southern edge of the *agora*, traders and moneylenders haggled over the terms of loan contracts. Before the Altar of the Twelve Gods at the north-center of the *agora*, two aristocrats bemoaned the costs of producing new tragedies, wondering aloud why they couldn't simply revive a masterwork as was done all around the countryside. And at Stoa Poikile, or the Painted Stoa, a more modest colonnade spanning the north edge of the public space, sophists and philosophers lectured at, and debated with, anyone willing to join in.

Some hours later, after wandering about and introducing himself to Athenians renowned as men of influence,

Hippocrates felt pangs of hunger, a sign that it would soon be time for the end of work and the midday meal. He began strolling back towards the Bouleuterion as per the sleepy official's instructions when shouting from beyond the *agora* grabbed his attention. Moments later, a squad of guard troops, shields and spears in hand, darted in loose formation westward towards the Dipylon gate. Hippocrates followed at a distance, curious about the commotion.

The troops had arranged themselves in a semicircle around the gateway, shields and spears locked as if readying for battle. Behind the troops was a line of archers, arrows pointed dead ahead. In front of the gathered forces, guards of the gate shouted at an onrush of people – men of all ages, women, and children – swarming into the city from the beyond the state graveyard.

"Stay in a straight line!" hollered one guard.

"No one gets in by shoving!" yelled another.

"Get back in a line or our men will use force!" said a third.

"Servants with jugs of water are being sent out shortly!"

"You will still receive rations if you aren't admitted by sunset!"

"Use the designated pits lining the wall if you have need of a latrine!"

It was a scene Hippocrates strained to process. He'd known that Athens could see its share of rowdy crowds, but never outside the weeks of a festival. And this was no festive gathering – no dancing, no chanting, no ecstasy on anyone's face. No, this was a horde of women with children and elderly men: disheveled peasants wearing unmatched jewelry; burly servants carrying wood doors; young women lugging sacks of diapers and tableware; and spinsters struggling to stay upright.

Refugees, in numbers at least as great if not greater than the ordinary population of the city.

"Asklepiad!" Hippocrates looked skyward. A watchtower guard was waving him to climb the gate for a chat. Hippocrates searched around briefly, discovering the stairway up the tower.

"Aristophanes?" said Hippocrates. "I thought only archers were stationed atop the towers. And weren't you at Piraeus?"

"We march back and forth to the city all the time. The generals like to proclaim it's for fitness. Between you and me it's for optics...makes the assembly think there are more of us standing guard all day than there really are."

Hippocrates looked down at the crowd. There was hardly room to breathe as far as a quarter a mile behind the gate, so many people were packed in by the graves. "Where did the refugees come from?"

"You think this is bad? You should have been at the gate by the south end of the city two days ago. What you see down there is an abandoned village by comparison."

"Why? Why are so many peasants pushing into the city?"

"Nobody told you about Olympian Pericles' master strategy?"

"My companions aren't Athenian, so no."

"Oh, what a plan it is! Since Athens can't hope to match the Spartans in a hoplite battle, Pericles ordered all of Attica to evacuate and settle behind the city walls through the campaign season. The Spartans, in turn, will march right on through the countryside, burning every farm and olive grove in their path..."

"...so the peasants can return home to a wasteland come winter solstice? That's madness."

"But you haven't heard the counter-strategy to make it all worthwhile! While the Spartans ravage our countryside, we're going to sail our fleet around the Peloponnese and lay waste to their ports and cities. If all goes well, the Spartans and their allies will starve and surrender before we do."

Hippocrates blankly, aghast and in disbelief.

"And let's just hope mighty Pericles doesn't venture off himself on too many of those expeditions," said Aristophanes. "If you think his strategy needs work, wait until you hear what Cleon and his drift of demagogues have in mind. A drove of donkeys can't bray as loudly."

Hippocrates absently bade farewell and wandered back down the watchtower, observing the mass of people shoving its way into Athens. An aging woman, toothless with an embittered mien, foraged on the path for stray bits of dried fruit. A man past military age, his lips parched and bleeding, held back slaves as he guzzled a jug of water meant for a family of five. And two preteen boys, giggling with glee, took turns urinating into a temporary latrine, watching bits of excrement spray up and onto the ground.

Thousands upon thousands of refugees pouring in from the countryside. No dedicated housing. No projects to expand sanitation. Rationing of staple foods. *The diseases we treat are brought on by changes in the air, in the water, by what we eat and drink...*

"Athens," said Hippocrates in abject dismay, "what are you doing?"

SEVENTEEN

Onesimos paced in frustration, watching the temple priests whisper in the ears of his slave investments, while attendants tried to cool their feverish, livid outsides with moist cloths. In hindsight, he wished he hadn't bothered offering to get these wretches the attention of a healer. Setting aside the direct costs of consulting the healers at the temple in Piraeus – fruits for votive offerings, livestock for sacrifice – getting these would-be miners treatment was costing him dearly. "Losing sleep and an entire round trip's worth of time," he grumbled to the night air.

Piraeus late at night was quieter and seedier than Athens. With so many slaves to perform the hard labor, the "good and beautiful" upper crust of Athenian society – the *kalokagathia*

– spent their nights drinking at *symposia* or in the company of courtesans. As a commercial and military port, Piraeus exuded a working-class ethos. There were drunks in the streets to be sure, but none that had time for philosophy or high-minded debate about the war. And a "gentleman's club" in Piraeus was the ironic label for a brothel full of slave-girls. Onesimos had his preferred spots and preferred girls, but this night he was having none of it.

When the first light of dawn creeped up on the horizon, Onesimos grabbed the attention of the head priest. "Has there been any change?"

"The best I can tell is they will survive," said the priest. "I've not seen men cursed this way, languishing in perpetual fever and perpetual thirst, no matter what we do. The good news is that none are purging themselves of blood, as you say happened to the one on your boat some months ago."

"And the bad news?"

"We've performed all the rituals and said all the traditional prayers over the sacrifice. Apollo has not yet returned these men to strength. And the curse has spread through their bodies. Two of them have some form of leprosy in one or two toes, and a third shows signs of the disease in his privy area."

"So now what? I simply wait for the gods to answer your prayers? We amputate the leprous extremities? Surely there must be something else I can try. My livelihood depends on these men being able to labor in the mines."

"The will of the gods cannot be rushed, Onesimos."

"The will of the gods..." said Onesimos, rolling his eyes. "Are there other temples to Apollo or Asklepios elsewhere in Attica?"

"There are," said the priest, "but I have absolute trust in our practice of the faith here. I have but one other suggestion. Not long ago, after the winter rains ceased, a fleet from the Chalcidice brought a physician here, on his way to Athens. Rumor has it he's a descendant of Asklepios himself. His stay was brief, but he treated half of the garrison for various injuries and ailments. He might have insights into medicine that lie beyond the purview of the gods."

"What's his name?"

Hippocrates thanked Thaïs for fetching his collected notes as he stood over the four slaves, watching them toss and turn on lambskins. The slaves had languished in the *enkoimeterion* for two days since bring dragged on carts into Athens.

"Still nothing?" said Onesimos.

"No significant change, at least none that's been sustained for more than an hour or two," said Hippocrates. "They're eating, drinking, and producing urine, all positive signs. I'm told one of them woke up in the night, disoriented but responsive to basic hand signals, rather than being outright delirious. If your translator were on call I might have a better feel for their progress on an hour-to-hour basis."

"I left him with my ship for now. I'll be honest, Asklepiad. I can't afford to keep these men here much longer. Can you cure them or not?"

"Nature, not medicine, holds the cure. Medicine only molds the body, so nature might do its work. These men felt overheated, so we rested them on lambskin leathers in the shade to keep them cool. Their mouths were parched, so we gave ample water to drink. I plan to go through my archived notes, trying to find a similar condition I might have treated in the past, but there are no guarantees. Is there something more you can tell me? Any unusual wind patterns on the sail from Naucratis? Unseasonal cold or rains in their home village?"

"I don't look to the weather for anything other than the day's sailing conditions, and I've been back and forth too many times to remember one trip to the next. I'll ask my crew if any of them kept a log of day-by-day winds or rains." Onesimos threw up his arms. "Do what you can, Asklepiad. I have some banking arrangements to make in the *agora*."

Hippocrates leafed through his scrolls, poring over each record for advice on what to try. Herophon, with acute fevers...no, his fevers came with chills and these men feel insufferably hot. Silenius with fever, loin pains, and discharges...no, his symptoms came from drink and overexertion. The wife of Philinus...she had a delirium like this group of slaves, but took with convulsions, and it was too close to childbirth to think the cause was anything else. Erasinus that lived by the gully...his symptoms were similar to those of the slaves, but he died in short order...no help there.

It didn't add up. Hippocrates had seen clusters of illness many times before, usually where men were housed together in tight quarters. Military encampments were notorious for the rapid spread of illness, and he'd even seen an entire *polis* fall ill over a course of days. But there was always something about the environment to explain the disease – a season of harsh wind conditions, standing water, spoiled foodstuffs. This group of slaves had fallen ill with similar, if not the same symptoms as their countrymen, in different places and at different times. Weather couldn't explain it, nor the condition of the water, nor any peculiarity of the local diet. There was a new, fundamental truth about the nature of disease that the Art was trying to reveal. But what?

Some hours later, Hippocrates had nodded off. As evening fell over the crude infirmary, he felt a tap on his shoulder jarring him awake. "Yes? Who's there?" he said, before his eyes came into focus.

A man in a priestly garment spoke in a raspy whisper. "Sorry, Asklepiad. I've come from the temple to Apollo in Piraeus. The slaves you tend to now were under our care not three days ago. I've come with four of my temple attendants, all with violent retching and a confusion bordering on madness. They complain of burning inside, day and night. One went as far as to dunk his head in our cistern of rainwater, hour after hour, with no relief. I've done all I can to no avail. Please, Asklepiad, I beg your expertise in finding a cure."

"Your voice is hoarse," said Hippocrates, pointing the men from Piraeus to what scant open space remained on the floor. "Is that a new problem?"

"Yes," said the priest. "I've also had some discomfort in the eyes."

"These attendants...did they complain of the same before the fits of retching began?"

"One did. I confess that I didn't ask the others."

Hippocrates stroked his beard, mulling over his limited space and dwindling supplies. "I'm going to recommend you join your attendants in staying here. I'll send word to Piraeus that nobody is to enter or leave your temple of Apollo, along with instructions on how to treat any man, woman, or child that falls ill."

"I don't understand. My voice is gone but I'm otherwise hale. Why keep me here like an invalid?"

"You're afflicted with the same disease process that attacked your attendants, the slaves you tended to at Piraeus, their fellow slaves at Lavrion, their brothers at the port of Naucratis, and whoever might live in the lands beyond Egypt at the end of the world. It's a disease not carried by the wind, nor borne by water. It's a disease that can't be cured by a rebalance of the humors nor any elixir I've studied."

The priest sat down on a rock, despondent. "Then we have angered the gods, and our offerings and hymns fall on deaf Olympian ears."

Hippocrates stood up and fired a stern look at the priest. "Men have been dying from this disease since at least before the winter rains. The condition migrates like a flock of birds, traversing rivers, seas, and large tracts of land. Whatever the will of the gods, when have they ever drawn out their ire over vast expanses of time and space? When have they ever wrought different degrees of misfortune, killing some within days and leaving others to wither? When have they ever punished both Greek and barbarian without obvious favor or malice, in both months of open warfare and months of retreat behind city walls? No, good priest, this disease is not the work of any god. But neither is it anything I can readily cure.

"I will do everything in my power to help you and your suffering attendants. But between the slaves and your party, I'm already running short on space. I've been granted the chance to speak before the assembly, and I'll urge Athens to build a bigger temple for a proper infirmary and school of medicine. But make no mistake, this is no mere poison or local miasma. This is a plague. If it continues to spread apace, it will create more widows and orphans than all the wars of man put together."

"Is there anything I might do to help?" said the priest.

"Follow my instructions to the letter," said Hippocrates. "Treat the work of the servants here as if it were my own hands guiding theirs. Help send word to every place of healing, and implore civic leaders to keep clean supplies and fresh water on hand for the sick."

"It's my honor to help, Asklepiad. Anything else?"

Hippocrates sighed in resignation. "Yes. Make offerings to win the favor of the gods."

EIGHTEEN

Hippocrates took a deep breath and glanced at Democritus and Gorgias, both returning a reassuring nod. "Athens!" he shouted. The thousands gathered on the Pnyx hillside silenced themselves and turned their attention to the visiting physician.

"Athens! Healing is a matter of time, but it is sometimes also a matter of opportunity. I stand before you, at the urging of your brothers, by the generosity of your elders, not to lecture but to present you an opportunity. Had I a wish to hold a lecture, the ambition is no laudable one. And should I depart my argument and cite the poets, I bid you take your leave, or at least exile me back to my home. To quote the poets argues feeble industry, and I forbid in medical practice an industry not pertinent to the Art and laboriously far-fetched.

"For we physicians take the lead in what is necessary for health. Left to themselves patients sink through their painful condition, give up the struggle and depart this life. But he who has taken the sick man in hand, if he display the discoveries of the Art, preserving nature, not trying to alter it, will sweep away the present depression or the distrust of the moment. For the healthy condition of a human being is a nature that has naturally attained a movement, not alien but perfectly adapted, by complete regimen and by everything combined.

"It is the business of the physician to know, in the first place, things similar and things dissimilar, those connected with things most important, most easily known, and in anywise known: which are to be seen, touched, and heard; which are to be perceived in the sight, and the touch, and the hearing, and the nose, and the tongue, and the understanding; and which are to be known by all the means we know things.

"The physician must know the things relating to surgery: the operator; the assistants; the light; where and how; how many things; where the body; the time, the manner, and the place. As to the instruments, he must know when and how they should be prepared, when and how they will be treated of afterwards.

"The physician must know to treat fractures, to attend to the length, breadth, thickness, and number of the compresses; the temperature and quantity of the water used; the presentation of the injured part, regulated according to nature.

"The physician must know of those symptoms beforehand, without being informed of them by the patient, which are of vital importance; the varieties of each complaint and their manifold divisions; where each species of symptom constitutes such a variety or a disease entity worthy to receive a different name; and if the remedies had been good and suitable to the complaints in which they are recommended.

"For my part, I approve of paying attention to everything relating to the Art. Those things which can be done well or properly should all be done properly. Those that can be quickly done should be done quickly. Those that can be neatly done should be done neatly.

"But the people do not recognize the difference between the uncommon physician and the common attendant, and are rather disposed to commend and censure extraordinary remedies. Thus the common people cannot, of themselves, form a judgement how diseases should be treated.

"While the Art knows no bounds in either place or time, its god-gifted precepts being timeless and perpetual in nature, its practice and continuity must necessarily lie in the terminable and ephemeral hands of man. I say, then, if Athens be the imperishable monument to glory, surely she must needs be the imperishable monument to the Art. If Athens be the eternal School of Greece, surely she is the rightful place for the enduring School of the Art.

"I beseech you, men of Athens and brothers of Greece, to seize this opportunity. Build an infirmary, a school of medicine, and a temple of healing. Build a monument to Apollo the Healer, to Asklepios, and to Hygieia and Panacea. Build a place of recuperation, of education, and of consecration. Build, that the Art shall be defined and determined by the splendor of Athens and the will of her people, now and for all time!"

The assembly returned to its ordinary buzz of voices, awaiting the next speaker. "Fine speech," said Democritus, patting his friend on the back. "You left out the part about the contagion, though. Was that intentional?"

"Word hasn't reached me of any new cases," said Hippocrates. "A proper infirmary and school of medicine will take months, even years to build anyways. No sense in creating undue panic."

Democritus turned to Thucydides, who'd advocated on the physician's behalf. "Do you think they'll bite?"

"No way to tell anymore," said Thucydides. "The assembly used to be as predictable as the phases of the moon. Some clans would vote one way, others the opposite, with

Pericles and the generals swaying things in the direction they needed to go. Before this war, spending the silver to build a grand temple and infirmary would have gone ahead without question. One of the aristocrats would have put up the funds on the orders of the King Archon. Your address would have been a formality, an exercise in mutual admiration."

"And now?" said Hippocrates.

"Take a look around," said Thucydides. "There are at least nine thousand men here, where a peacetime quorum was barely six thousand. They're raucous, volatile...treating each issue and each vote as a battle of wills, a winner-take-all contest between those that side with the aristocrats and those that side with the democrats."

The densest part of the crowd scattered, making room for the purposeful stride of a man making his way to the speaker's platform.

"Who's that plowing through the crowd? He's not wearing a general's helmet," said Hippocrates.

The gruff man took the platform. Bare-chested, he wore his garment tied around his waist, defying the formal tradition of wrapping it over the shoulder. Large swaths of the crowd roared in cheers, while others in attendance turned their backs in revulsion.

"That," said Thucydides with a sneer, "is Cleon, son of Cleaenetus. He's no general."

"I've heard about this man," said Hippocrates.

"As have I," said Democritus. "He has quite the reputation. What did he do to win such favor – and fervor – among the popular crowd?"

"Nothing of note," said a disgusted Thucydides, and left the assembly without uttering one more word.

"An infirmary!" yelled Cleon. "An infirmary, a temple, a school is what we need...so says this...this foreigner. We, the citizens of Athens, retreating – no, cowering behind our walls – now have need of an infirmary? For what casualties? What wounds?

"For the second year now, the leadership of this mighty *polis*, this mighty empire, has deemed that we Athenians should cloister ourselves and hide like piteous cowards. We do nothing to protect our borders from the ravages of other peoples. We do nothing to show our strength and grow our prosperity. We do nothing to reinforce old alliances and form new ones, that we might face down and vanquish our enemy.

"And those bold and fearless legions, those awesome imposing warships...where are they? Frittering the days and squandering our treasures, laying siege on distant shores. Their victories have not been your victories, their triumphs have not been your triumphs. And while they idly celebrate hither and yon, waiting for their quarry to starve and submit, what cause to celebrate have your families?"

Those close to the platform began stomping their feet like drums of war, building to a crescendo while Cleon paused, as if to feed off the malignant energy of the assembly.

"Might I suggest we take our leave, Asklepiad?" said Gorgias.

"Forget voting on a temple and infirmary. They're on the brink of a riot," said Democritus.

Laches, son of Melanopos, and Nicias, son of Niceratus, two of the *strategoi*, ascended the platform and began to bicker with Cleon as the din of the angry crowd grew. "Athenians, stay your impulses!" said Nicias. "We have placed our faith in Pericles and he has not led us astray! Even now, our fleet lays waste to the shores of the Peloponnese. This war will be won, not by angry words but by the patient use of force."

"Look beyond the city walls," said Cleon. "See the pillars of smoke rising from the north! Again the Spartans set your fields afire! Again the Spartans take axes to your groves! Again they march from township to township, to rape and enslave your brothers and wives too brave to cower! And again your leaders reduce the urgency of war into a pointless exercise in patience. I say we give this...this physician some wounds to sew and fractures to set! I say we muster our arms and sally to meet the Spartans in open combat! Who stands with me?"

A chant from the younger members of the assembly grew to a crescendo. "Fight now! Fight now!" By the dozens, then the hundreds, men of the assembly left the Pnyx to march through the streets of Athens.

Nicias pushed Cleon off the platform. "Guard captains! Cut off the protesters from the gates and direct your men to disperse the crowds! Recall the garrison from the Piraeus for backup!"

"So much for a new infirmary," said Democritus with a shrug.

"The infirmary," said Hippocrates, his voice trailing off. "Come with me now."

"Why?" said Democritus.

"If that mob marches through the temple, it risks spreading the plague to all corners of the city. If that happened, burning all of Attica to the ground would be a gift from the gods by comparison."

NINETEEN

The sixteenth day of Munichion, morning of the full moon closest to the spring equinox, could not have been more perfect for a festival procession. The cloudless sky, the warm shade of the hillside grove, the invigorating whiff of briny maritime air on a deep breath...pity the girls were too young to appreciate it, thought Hypatia, priestess of Artemis. Still, the sight of frolicking, innocent Athenian girls, none older than nine, tripping over too-long yellow robes, was a tonic for Hypatia's nerves, frayed nearly to the point of breaking on the walk from Athens the day before.

Athens had grown busier, rowdier, and filthier by the day. Leading the other priestesses and children down the Long Walls from Athens to Piraeus proved more agitating than the interminable hours at the loom she remembered from her younger days. With every home in Athens jammed with houseguests, and every public building now a makeshift inn for farmers' families, the city alleys and Long Walls had become a refugee camp for the wretched and impoverished of the countryside. Every few steps meant another beggar to evade or cesspit to sidestep. The stifling crowd and stench of human waste poisoned the air in the heat of midday. No place for children, least of all daughters of the noble families, but the ritual of the Munichia came first. And awful as the walk might have been, the sanctuary of the goddess by the minor port remained free of people. Besides, winning the favor of Artemis was worth the discomfort, especially with the peoples of Greece at war.

Despite the importance of the equinox to the planting season, or perhaps because of it, the Munichia was a relatively minor festival for the Athenians. The tradition was barely a half-century old, enacted to commemorate the victory over Persia at Salamis. But as the years passed and the immediacy of the war faded from memory, the Munichia had become something of a warm-up for young Athenian girls...a dress rehearsal for their initiation into womanhood that would come later in childhood.

As they marched uphill to the temple, Hypatia smacked a beat on her priestly scepter, leading the children in a song adapted from the revered dramatist Aeschylus' play about the Persians' defeat. "Okay, children, you've practiced this for weeks.

"That once was Persia's, lieth in the dust!
Woe on the man who first announceth woe—
Yet must I all the tale of death unroll!
Hark to me, Persians! Persia's host lies low.
As one who saw, by no loose rumor led,
Lords, I would tell what doom was dealt to us."

With another priestess working to herd the youngest of the bunch, the girls chanted in response as the chorus from the staged play,

"Alack, how vainly have they striven!
Our myriad hordes with shaft and bow
Went from the Eastland, to lay low
Hellas, beloved of Heaven!"

"Wonderful!" said Hypatia. "Let's continue.

"Piled with men dead, yea, miserably slain,
Is every beach, each reef of Salamis!
Their bows availed not! all have perished, all,

By charging galleys crushed and whelmed in death.

Out on thee, hateful name of Salamis,

Out upon Athens, mournful memory!"

The children answered in unison,

"Woe upon this day's evil fame!

Thou, Athens, art our murderess;

Alack, full many a Persian dame

Is left forlorn and husbandless!"

The procession reached the temple atop the hillock. The oldest girls in the group, their faces hidden behind bear masks, performed the *arkteia*, a dance around the altar on slow tiptoe to a tune played on flute, mimicking the lope of a bear. The younger girls encircled the altar inside the dancers, offering rounded cakes with lit candles to the goddess. Hypatia ushered a goat to the altar. Muttering a soft hymn, she slit the goat's throat in the final act of the ritual, letting blood seep inside cracks of the marble temple floor. While the girls danced on and ate cakes, she and her fellow priestesses worked quickly to carve up the carcass for a festival meal that night, burning the fat and entrails for Artemis' share.

One of the dancers, seven-year-old Eudokia, dropped out of her circle and approached Lysandra, one of the other priestesses. "Priestess? I feel sick."

"Have you felt like this for long?" said Lysandra. "Do you feel tired or thirsty?"

"No. My head is hot and my mouth hurts to swallow," said Eudokia.

"Oh dear," said Lysandra. She drew a water-skin from a sack she'd carried and bent to get a closer look at her young charge. "Have a drink, my dear, and...oh my!"

"What is it?" said Hypatia, looking up from the meat cutting.

"Her eyes are red as blood," said Lysandra.

Eudokia began to cry and retch. "What's going on?!?" She had a fit of loud, hoarse coughs, then sobbed uncontrollably. "Did I do wrong? What did I do, Priestess?!?"

"No, no, you were wonderful!" said Lysandra, clutching the girl in a tight hug.

Hypatia wore an uneasy smile. "My child, Artemis does not punish young girls that honor her the way you've done." The other girls stopped what they were doing and gathered to comfort their friend. "The way you've all done, my children. This is a normal thing that girls get...maybe from too much dancing in the heat. And the redness Lysandra sees in your eyes is a gift! Artemis is so pleased with your dancing and singing, she painted your eyes in her favorite color!"

Eudokia returned the priest's smile and calmed down. Lysandra directed the children to gather their things for a walk back down the hill. They'd spend a night in Piraeus then brave the Long Walls again the next day.

As the girls trundled downhill, Hypatia pulled the other priestess aside. "There are legions of slaves new to Piraeus. I'll arrange for two or three of them to take Eudokia back to Athens in a cart tonight, once the others fall asleep. Give the girls wine with their supper, that they might fall asleep early."

"As you wish," said the priestess. "But why send the girl home in the night?"

"Eudokia carries a contagion that shuttered the temple to Apollo. I dare not raise the ire of Artemis by letting the disease strike her sanctuary too."

Crowding the doorway, Aecus gazed wistfully in the moonlit eyes of Xanthias, his student and beloved young friend. "Xanthias, you don't look yourself at all. Were you not up for company this evening?"

Aecus had spotted the youth years earlier in the streets, lithe and graceful even in horseplay. He was always the one, Aecus mused, and by the gods the courtship was worth it. Rubbing him in oil at the boxing grounds while humming words of encouragement, wrestling a rival suitor to the ground, sleeping at the father's doorstep that rainy winter night...all to win the right to mold the boy's natural vigor into the sexual confidence befitting an Athenian man.

Xanthias returned a warm but labored smile. "It's always a delight to spend time with you, Teacher. You've taught me so much about philosophy, love, and the life of a citizen. I just feel ill. Not like the normal catarrhs that come and go within days. This is a misery I've never felt before."

"There's a symposium at the home of Prodicus tonight," said Aecus. "I was hoping to introduce you some of my acquaintances."

"I don't believe wine will do me any good, Teacher," said Xanthias, "and I don't have the strength for dancing and games."

Aecus strode forward. Reaching with the left hand, he caressed Xanthias under the chin. "Forget the party, then." Aecus extended his right hand to fondle the youth's genitals.

"No, no, please no. I have no appetite for intimacy, even if only between the thighs."

"Kiss me, then, and I'll leave." Xanthias acquiesced. As their lips locked, Aecus suddenly pushed back and spat at the ground. "Your mouth tastes like blood! Your breath is foul!"

"I told you I didn't feel well," said Xanthias, his voice hoarsening. He collapsed in the older man's arms, weak and delirious with fever.

The *gymnasiarch* wore a puzzled look. His star wrestler, Androkles, lay on the dirt in a cold sweat, having taken a third pin in stunningly short order. It was Androkles' first loss in over a year – against a smaller opponent no less – in a key warm-up tournament before the major contest at the height of summer's Panathenaea festival.

"Androkles!" shouted the *gymnasiarch*. His charge sauntered over, seeming dazed and surprisingly winded, given his lackluster effort. "Did someone pay you to throw the bout? What happened out there?"

Androkles lazily brushed dirt off his oiled arms and torso. "I don't know, Sir. I've had one lousy night's sleep after another this week, with a gods-awful taste in my mouth." He dunked his head in a rainwater pot to cool off, then scooped water to his mouth in a desperate thirst. "I just stepped inside the square and suddenly felt drained of all strength. I could barely see straight after he pinned me a second time."

"Did you not eat last night or this morning? You don't look like you've dropped a weight class."

"No change to my diet or my schedule, Sir. I haven't been goofing off in practice either. I've been here every day at sunrise for three weeks. Not a day missed since returning from Lavrion."

"How's your father doing? Does he have enough hours in the day to count all the silver he's digging up?"

"On the sail back from the mines, I believe he said, 'If your trainer asks how I'm doing, tell that oily-skinned sweat monger I've already set aside funds for every tournament this year.'"

The *gymnasiarch* laughed. "He's a good man. He believes in you, same as me...you're the next Milo of Croton, a people's champion in the making."

Androkles shrugged. "If you say so, Sir."

"I'm serious. Once you do your two years' service as an *ephebe* in the military, it's time to make you a full-time athlete. The Isthmian, the Nemean...even the Olympiad. You're the best I've seen in a generation. In my prime I couldn't have pinned you, and you haven't even hit your peak muscle size."

"Thank you, Sir."

"Now go wash off and get some food." The *gymnasiarch* gave Androkles a stiff pat on the back and went on to watch the next bout.

Androkles felt the cold sweat and malaise move down into his lower belly, followed by an intense cramp. Maybe he'd eaten a bad cut of meat for supper the previous night after all, and just didn't notice. He found his way to the latrine to relieve himself before a bath.

Two years of border guard service and training, then time to become a full-time athlete, he repeated back to himself. Wow! Classical wrestling was insanely popular around Greece, with a pantheon of champions tracing all the way back to Heracles. It was the ultimate test of strength, leverage, and pure force of will. Any half-decent fighter could win tournaments and fame at *pankration*, freestyle fighting that allowed punches, kicks, and bites. But to make it as a wrestler, after all the years of training and prayers...to wow the crowds, maybe make the semi-finals – even win! – one of the pan-Hellenic tournaments...talk about a dream come true.

A wave of intense nausea overcame Androkles as he evacuated his bowels. He felt a rush of hot fluid escape his lower body, a few seconds of vertigo, then everything went black.

Not long thereafter, he was found prone on the dirt and not breathing, a track of blood running from the latrine up to his muscular thighs and backside.

I dragged myself out of bed for this, Philocleon moaned to himself. He rolled the lead token between the fingers of his right hand, itching for the instant he could redeem it for his pittance of a juror's pay and go back home. It was the last case on the day's schedule, and he could barely bring himself to care about the outcome.

Like most of the six thousand-strong pool of jurors, Philocleon was retired, a cobbler who'd passed his trade and shop onto his son. Among Pericles' many reforms to the democracy was the institution of pay for jurors of the popular courts. It was only half of a standard day's pay, Philocleon reminded himself, but still better than getting an achy back and achier backside for nothing.

Each morning, jurors were randomly assigned by the hundreds to the various court buildings in and around downtown Athens. In theory and practice, it made a jury impossible for a litigant to bribe, even if the presiding magistrate was open to graft. But it belied an uncomfortable reality: the jury tended to side with the most convincing talker, rather than any moral or ethical ideal of justice. It opened a huge market for the slick tongues and slicker prose of the sophists...but Philocleon saw right through it.

What could be more painful than what he was sitting through at that moment? A sharecropper with nary a pot to piss in, garbling words written by some pederast poet-philosopher, pounding his fist in the air as though the location of his olive tree was a matter of national security. What drivel.

Philocleon felt a tickle in his throat and barked out a hard cough, breaking the speaker's concentration and drawing the attention of many fellow jurors. Was this a continuation of the same symptoms that laid him up for three days, or had he come down with something new?

He coughed again, a few times in succession, drawing the attention of the trial magistrate. The magistrate fired an irate glare at Philocleon and ordered the speaker's water clock reset.

Within minutes, Philocleon resumed coughing, now uncontrollably, straining against an unquenchable fire in his chest. Without bothering to be discrete, he pushed his way along the jury bench, gasping for open air away from the crowded courthouse. Staff in hand, he hacked and retched all the half-mile trek home, his pace hampered by throngs of squealing children and napping refugees in every road and alleyway.

Once home, the scoured his belonging for anything to help the symptoms abate. Wine, honey, cheeses, ointments...nothing seemed to arrest the spasms of cough nor ease the tortured burning in his chest. After an hour without success, and choked of his breath, he stepped back into the streets, crying for help. Unable to shout above the din of the overcrowded *polis*, he collapsed soon thereafter, crying and coughing blood, until death finally claimed him.

TWENTY

Hippocrates chugged his cupful of wine to the cheers of his friends. How many was this? Six? Eight? And gods, did it ever go to his head...what self-respecting Greek drank wine this strong? "Did you not cut this with any water?" He said.

"There is no such thing as water!" said Gorgias, who'd won the roll of the dice and was the evening's appointed drinks-master.

"So what is it I've been pissing out all day?" said Democritus.

"If there is water, nothing can be known about it," said Gorgias.

"No philosophy!" said Hippocrates and Democritus in unison.

"Fine," said Gorgias. "I shall enchant you all with a retelling of my adventures in Sarmatia, distant land of the warrior—"

"We've heard it!" said Democritus. "You're getting forgetful in your age, Teacher. You, young man...can you play the lyre?"

A servant handed the instrument and plectrum to Aristophanes. "With wine on board, who knows?" He picked a few notes. "Haven't played in a few years, but I should be able to strum something simple. What's it strung to?"

"Dorian, base tone and scale," said the servant.

Aristophanes played a familiar children's song. "Nice." He plucked out the refrain from a common folk dance. "I might make a mistake here or there, but anyone want to call out a request?"

"We'll do better than that," said Democritus. "Play whatever comes to you or improvise something for a dance." He picked up a hand drum and smacked it with his palm a few times. "Euthalia!"

As Aristophanes started into another song, Euthalia and Thaïs twirled into the room, performing the veil dance Hippocrates had caught them practicing weeks earlier. The women were adorned in matching hairstyles, makeup, and translucent gowns – this time tailored for both. Euthalia clapped a beat on castanets dangling at her wrists to keep her protégé in step, not that it was needed. Both danced spritely and artfully, circling the men's couches, using their silken veils to tease as any good courtesan would. Once Aristophanes played the final refrain, the men gave a roaring ovation as the women hugged in delight.

"I didn't know you had a *hetaera*," said Aristophanes.

"I don't," said Hippocrates, "she's with Democritus."

"Not the one with the breasts, the young one," said Aristophanes. "She's a blossom."

"Thaïs? No, no, she's not my *hetaera*." Even through the fog of intoxication, Hippocrates could decipher what Aristophanes was thinking. "And she's not a whore or slave, either. She's...she's my sister. And my personal assistant at the temple."

Democritus did a double-take and raised an eyebrow. Hippocrates fired back a glance with a message clear as day: shut up and play along.

"I had no idea, Asklepiad," said Aristophanes. "Your friends never spoke of a sister when I attended a *symposium* and they told me all about you. I know I was drunk, but I think I'd remember a detail like that."

"Speaking as an expert, wine does not do the memory good," said Hippocrates. "But Thaïs is really my half-sister, by my father's consort here in Athens. My father was away from Kos for months on end in my childhood. A man can only go so long without his needs being met, and the old man never cared for whores. One of his friends frequented the courtesans' hall, and one thing led to another."

"Well she is quite the attractive young woman. She'd make someone a very fine wife. If she can learn to run an *enkoimeterion*, running a household can't be hard."

Hippocrates grunted. He hadn't given much thought to any long-term plans for Thaïs. His domestic slaves had always seemed content, even growing up. Both he and his father had freed the odd farmhand over the years, and Hippocrates himself gave his blessing to more than one slave marriage. But he'd bartered for Thaïs out of concern for her safety, not any genuine household need.

She was entering her prime childbearing years, and Aristophanes had a point – she was sharp enough to make an excellent family manager. But if Hippocrates freed the girl, she had neither family nor property...what man of noble birth would marry her without a name or dowry behind her? Could she train as a *hetaera*? She hadn't the cultured upbringing, and would that not condemn her to the same fate she faced when they met? It would be a shame to confine her to the laundry and the loom until old age, however.

Without sensing the passage of time, Hippocrates was barely staying awake. This was his first night of relaxation and fun since leaving Kos so many months earlier. Too much wine and not enough water, he thought with a grin, as sleep finally arrived. Democritus would poke him periodically, in a vain effort to rouse the unresponsive physician, but before long all the symposium attendants were snoring away, oblivious even to the rising sun.

At mid-morning, Hippocrates' need for rest was losing the battle of wills with his stomach and bladder. His friends still unconscious, he readied himself for his day of work at the temple, when a servant came running over.

"I'm sorry to disturb you, Physician," said the servant, "but now that you're awake, I have news from one of your infirmary attendants."

Hippocrates splashed water on his face. "No need to apologize. Go ahead."

"I bring word from Telemachos. He begs your attendance as soon as possible. The *enkoimeterion* is overrun with the sick – adults and children alike, from all corners of the city."

"Overrun? But things were fine when I left there just yesterday afternoon." He dressed in a clean garment, grabbed a handful of dried fruits, and rushed from the house.

The colonnade at the infirmary entrance was jammed with dozens of people in varying states of misery, some peaked and sickly, others hale but carrying ill children, pushing their way forward. The priest from Piraeus was at their head, trying to organize the crowd and calm their simmering anger.

Hippocrates found a boulder to climb atop. "Telemachos! Telemachos!" He made eye contact with several of his students, that helped him squeeze through the crowd. "What's happened here? Where did all these people come from?"

"They arrived just after dawn, Asklepiad," said Telemachos. "The priest said that you were familiar with the disease and could offer help."

Hippocrates waved the priest over. "Did you not follow my advice and instructions?"

"To the letter, Asklepiad," said the priest. "But every public building in Piraeus is crammed with the sick and dying."

"Why wait so long to notify me?" said Hippocrates.

"We sent word to the civic leadership, both at the port and here in Athens proper. We also related your instructions around quarantine. As I understand, the guard at the gate to the Long Walls was doubled, and the sentries were given specific instructions not to let any more refugees into the city. These people grew desperate, as did I, so I led them here on religious authority. But the guards only let so many through."

"What do you mean, only so many of you?"

"This is but a small number of the people that have fallen ill, Asklepiad. Piraeus is rife with the afflicted, and the death toll climbs by the hour."

"If the public buildings are full, where is everyone else?"

"As I said, the city guard put a limit on who they let pass."

"Gods," said Hippocrates, his voice trailing off. He darted as best he could through the mid-morning crowd of the *agora*, weaving and shoving his way to the Piraean Gate. He spoke briefly with the sentries and climbed a watchtower that overlooked the Long Walls corridor. Thousands of sick refugees from Piraeus wrestled with the homeless for square cubits of space and rations of water. Fights erupted everywhere, this one over a scrap of food, that one over an overfull cesspit. And everyone pushed headlong into Athens, desperate for a bed and the attention of a healer.

Shaken and horrified, Hippocrates sauntered back to the *agora*, and pounded on the door of the Tholos. A bewildered city magistrate opened the door. "Can I help you?"

"My lord *prytanis*, I'm Hippocrates, son of Heraclides, Physician of Kos. I must speak to the leadership of Athens on a matter of urgency."

"Does this matter pertain to a possible death by homicide or to the security of the *polis*?"

"Both," said Hippocrates, "and I swear by Apollo the Healer and by Asklepios, there isn't a minute to waste."

TWENTY-ONE

Hippocrates was both dumbfounded and dismayed, at a loss as to where to direct the stream of refugees, each more violently sick than the last. The whole of spring had passed since the ill-mannered slave trader had arrived in Athens, the pestilence in tow. Every day brought word of another public building overrun with children clinging to life, another barracks of miserable soldiers, another family carted to its grave. Hippocrates had lost track of the plague's spread and death toll. It had become so ubiquitous and uncontrollable, there was simply no point in tallying up the numbers of infirmed or dead. He, his student physicians, and a corps of commandeered temple workers spent their days racing inside the walls of Athens and her ports. He'd recruited soldiers too, battle medics to patch up the wounded. Not an hour passed when a child didn't show up at the temple, wailing from the pain of a broken arm or distaste of a bloodied mouth, as Athenians beat one another for rations or valuables pilfered from the houses of the dead.

They did what they could, providing symptom relief to the afflicted and seeing to the safety of the widowed and orphaned. But many of Hippocrates' assistants felt the sting of the plague themselves, a handful succumbing to its fatal touch.

He surveyed the temple that was his improvised infirmary. Attendants walked on tiptoes to avoid injuring the tightly packed refugees. Many of the sick were delirious, moaning and retching blood into their stripped garments. Others, mainly women and youth, curled up in terror, traumatized by the wanton violence of a city losing its grip on decency and order. Still others, writhing and gasping, crawled to a latrine pit to relieve themselves, using what little strength they could muster to bury their filth with dirt. The attendants then followed with pails of sea water for cleaning, and ladles of spring water for drink.

Hippocrates' growing despair was broken by the rhythmic march of armed troops, a retinue to herald the visit of the Athenian generals Hagnon, son of Nicias, Cleopompus, son of Clinias, and Phormio. What now? Hippocrates exchanged terse greetings with the three commanders, then caught a subtle nod from Aristophanes, smirking from amid the entourage.

"We'll get straight to the point, Asklepiad," said Phormio. "Have you had any luck in curing the contagion?"

"No, Commander," said Hippocrates. "The death toll continues to rise, even accelerate, by the day."

"Have you devised a way to limit its spread at least?" said Cleopompus.

"Sadly no," said Hippocrates. "Applying basic principles relieves symptoms in some people, but the disease continues to spread with a virulence I've not heard of nor read about ever before."

"The contagion followed me to Potidaea," said Hagnon. "I lost more than a thousand hoplites of the four thousand stationed there. We were there a month with nothing to show for it but the ash heaps of a thousand funeral pyres."

"Tell us what you know, Asklepiad," said Phormio. "Is Athens battling the gods as well as Sparta?"

"Only poets and oracles know the ways of the gods, Commander," said Hippocrates. "The disease affects the head first, much like an ordinary seasonal contagion, only with more severe symptoms – extreme irritation of the throat, bleeding from the mouth, eyes flush with blood, and so on. From there it moves through the whole of the body, first to the throat and chest with a cough, then the stomach and innards with retching and vomiting. Death is not common at this point, but not unheard of...it depends largely on the constitution of the patient. The very young and very old are most likely to succumb in this stage.

"There is a feeling of intense heat inside the body, yet no obvious fever. Some will strip themselves bare, even on the coolest of nights. Others will complain of an unquenchable thirst or immerse themselves in cisterns of rainwater. The disease ends its course in a blood-soaked purge...blood from the mouth, blood in the vomit, and the bloodiest of stools. Only the fittest can survive these late stages of the illness. Even then, some discover boils and ulcers that linger in the private parts, while others are struck with amnesia of the entire episode."

"How have you managed to escape death?" said a stone-faced Phormio.

"A curious question, Commander," said Hippocrates. "Not by any chicanery or sorcery, I assure you."

"We ask only for the sake of our troops and the security of the *polis*, Asklepiad," said Hagnon. "We mean no disrespect."

Hippocrates sighed. "I've avoided death but not illness. I went through the early stage of the disease not long after the crowds from Piraeus pushed through here. I guessed – and it was only a guess – that the contagion spreads by contact with the unclean discharges of its victims. A shared goblet of water, use of a common latrine, even sexual intercourse...any of these could be responsible for spread of the disease. I made it a point to limit any direct contact I might have with the acutely sick. The result was a few days of retching and chest discomfort on my part, but that was it. I've even been able to extend my hours treating the languid without a return of symptoms."

"So if not the cure, you've found a way to prevent it," said Cleopompus.

"Only to better the odds of prevention, not guarantee it," said Hippocrates. "Some of the elderly temple attendants took all the same precautions, and now lie interred in the public graveyards."

Phormio turned to Hagnon. "Will those suggestions suffice for your return campaign to Potidaea?"

Hippocrates interjected, "I'm sorry...that's what you wanted? Ideas for how you might come out victorious in your precious siege?"

"The needs of the military are not your concern, Asklepiad," said Phormio with a sneer. "Go back to your work, and I offer thanks for your insights."

"No!" said Hippocrates.

"I'm sorry?" said Phormio, all three generals standing in Hippocrates' face. "You have something to add?"

"We're not at your encampment, so you can't stifle me as insubordinate," said Hippocrates. "You want to know about this plague, that your contest with Sparta has wrought upon your beloved city? Sure, you, Pericles, the Archons, the leaders of the assembly...you can ignore the orchards of Attica that burn night and day. You can brush off the hordes of widows and peasants dying of plague. You can voice concern only for your precious citizen soldiers. But you will not dismiss the reality of this war and expect me to clean up the mess...not until you've seen everything endured by the people you claim to fight for."

As Cleopompus looked poised to draw his sword, Phormio held him back. "Alright, Asklepiad. I'll indulge your little grandstanding tantrum. But if you're wasting my time, I'll slit your throat myself, plague or no plague."

Hippocrates sent an assistant for bandages smeared with oils and ointments, and handed them out to the generals and guards.

"What's this?" asked Hagnon.

"A cloth bandage soaked in various aromatics," said Hippocrates. "Don't lose it. Now follow me to the tower overlooking the gate to the Long Walls."

Few Athenians had dared approach the Long Walls once the plague struck Athens with a vengeance. *Ephebes* and sentries either stood in the guard towers or maintained their watch on the ground from a distance. The miles of walkway between Athens and Piraeus had degenerated into an anarchic slum, a labyrinth of tents and ramshackle shelters dotted by overflowing cesspits. The moaning and retching of the afflicted filled the air, punctuated by the howls of mourners and sobbing pleas for help.

The generals stared down in silence. They saw old men muffle the cries of boys forced into sex between the thighs and outright rape, criminal affronts to the *pederaistia* traditions of noble Athenians. They watched women play tug-of-war with their husbands, as daughters were prostituted for rations of water. And they witnessed a brawl break out between teenagers, each jockeying to be the first to pile a body atop a makeshift pyre...to be rid of the remains of a dead parent before the onset of rot. But nothing could prepare the generals' men for the smell.

A fetid stench hung above the Long Walls, of urine and feces and vomit and sweat and carrion...and death. Corpses of the lonely, incompletely burned, untended bodies putrefying in their tents...it was air so noxious as to frighten off vermin looking to feed. Three of Phormio's guards gagged uncontrollably, Aristophanes among them, and Cleopompus stepped away to throw up.

"I've seen enough," said Phormio, muffled by the bandage held over his nose and mouth. He led the retinue back down the guard tower and into the city proper. "Cleopompus, summon every sentry in the city, including the *ephebes* and our personal guard, to meet in the *agora* within the hour. Before I arrive to address them, tell them this slave trader is to be arrested on sight, and laden with the heaviest chains our metalsmiths can forge. Ensure the same instructions are sent to the garrison at Piraeus, and whoever we have stationed near the Lavrion mines." Cleopompus bowed and led the entourage away. Phormio held out his sword. "Hagnon, take my sword in hand to the Strategeion. Tell Pericles you send word from me personally to call an urgent plenary meeting of the assembly."

Phormio watched his generals march off, then set a hand on Hippocrates' shoulder. "Athens owes you a debt, Hippocrates, and begs you to help her suffering citizens as best you can. If I might make one more request, I need your help in devising a plan to see these refugees moved, both for safety and to nurse as many back to health as is possible."

"It's my honor, Commander," said Hippocrates, "but what I suggest might not seem palatable to the citizens of the city."

"Suggest what you must, Asklepiad. We cannot fight a war for the glory of a graveyard."

TWENTY-TWO

Phormio's booming voice reduced the racket on the Pnyx to a murmur. At nine, perhaps ten thousand strong, the assembly of citizens was in a combustible mood. Rage, anguish, horror, panic...however extreme the emotion, it was palpable somewhere in the horde of grieving, incensed Athenians.

"I said that's enough!" said Phormio at the top of his lungs, bringing the murmur of the assembly to a hush. "I will not waste your time with rhetorical tricks or lengthy debates, nor insult the intelligence of anyone by pretending the situation is not dire. Each of you has been witness to the carnage wrought by this war, whether at the tip of a spear or the gateway to an infirmary. Each of you has lost a farmstead, a home, parent, a wife, a child, a brother, a brother-in-arms, or everyone and everything you held dear.

"As your elected generals, we foresaw the ravages of war but not those of the pestilence. For the first, the *strategoi* assume responsibility. For the second, we assume leadership to mitigate the devastation. This plague has brought fast ruin on the very meaning of a moderate life as the Athenian ideal. What crimes men of low character once perpetrated in the shadows are now brazenly carried out in the light of day. What cheer and good faith we once extended without hesitancy are now supplanted by suspicion and frank barbarism. It ends today!"

Phormio paused to let the gravity of his words suffuse the crowd. "The sentries and *ephebes* of the city have been directed to conduct a house-by-house census of sleeping space and take inventory of staple foodstuffs. Each of you shall welcome into his home all the refugees your space will allow, in the traditions and obligations of *xenia*, guest-friendship. Any shortfall in a household's food stores will be replenished by the public stores, under a fiscal arrangement to be debated and voted upon at the next regular meeting of the assembly.

"The public buildings and sanctuaries will be used as houses of healing, under the direction of the physician Hippocrates, son of Heraclides, of Kos. You shall heed his instructions as if the words were uttered by any Athenian magistrate or face a charge of treason at my behest. I now yield the platform to him."

Hippocrates nodded at Phormio in a gesture of thanks. "This pestilence has massacred your families and friends by the thousands, left indelible scars on the survivors, and broken the spirit of this indomitable city. The death toll climbs this very minute and will continue to climb for many days to come. To suggest otherwise would betray the core tenets of my Art, for blind affirmation and talk are deceptive and treacherous. But by the dynamism of this great city, I believe we can bring this scourge of Athens under a measure of control.

"What I propose will sound extreme, but for extreme diseases, extreme methods of cure are most suitable. Whatever the point of origin of this plague, its material essence propagates in the air, on the wind. None save the gods can drive the wind, but man does retain the means to alter its quality.

"Of the caustics employed in medicine, fire is the most powerful. Those diseases which medicines cannot cure, the knife cures. And those which the knife cannot cure, fire cures. Our ancient forebears and the old healers of Egypt used fire to cleanse the air of evil, both natural and supernatural. I am no priest, so I leave the cleansing of the spirit to the experts in the spiritual. But we can free Athens from the miasma – the stench of sickness and death – that poisons her skies. Will it rid you of this plague? No man can say. But a breathable air, free of toxin and pestilence, is the best hope for the body to find its way back to a healthy state. And apart from evacuating the city into the spearheads of Spartan invaders, it's the only idea I have left.

"I ask every Athenian – man, woman, and child – to gather every vial of perfume, every plank of fragrant wood, every leaf of aromatic herb, every jar of spice. Bring it to the *agora*. My assistants and I will light bonfires of incense in every corner of the city and feed the flames day and night with all manner of essence. By the energy of your spirit and the grace of the gods, we will do everything in our power to rid your city of disease and restore strength to your suffering loved ones."

"Take your gods-cursed plans to 'save us' and go to the crows!" came a familiar holler from the crowd. Pushing hard to the speaker's platform were the naked chest and brawny arms of Cleon, flanked by two of his compatriots.

"Cleon, I do not yield to you!" said Phormio.

"You've already yielded the platform to this physician," said Cleon, "and no foreigner will prevent me from exercising my right to speak to my fellow Athenians!" Phormio, fuming but speechless, stepped back. "This assembly gathers at a moment of crisis for our nation, but it is not the proximate crisis of plague. No, the problems we face now – pestilence and violence within our gates, debacle and devastation without – comprise a crisis of leadership and political will, a crisis that will fester so long as we lean on very same man that created it.

"Yes, I point at Pericles. It is a sad truth that ordinary men manage public affairs better than the gifted. The 'good and the beautiful' strive above all to appear wiser than the laws, to overrule every proposition brought forward. Yet by such behavior they bring ruin upon their country, subjugating the needs of the people to the whims of their intellectual vanity. Those who mistrust their own cleverness, though, are content to be less learned than the laws, and conduct business without falling prey to their own fancy. In which of these categories of men, the common or the elite, does mighty Pericles place himself?

"Doubtless the venerated general will look to place the blame upon you, the ordinary citizens. And that charge will indeed carry a degree of uncomfortable truth. The persons to blame are you, who are so foolish as to make governance a contest of cleverness, who indulge in an oration as you would take in a sight, slaves to the pleasure of the ear. You are easy victims of new-fangled arguments, unwilling to follow received conclusions that lay themselves bare. Yet by being quick in catching an argument you are slow in foreseeing its consequences.

"Do not be traitors to yourselves, but recall as nearly as possible this moment of suffering. Breathe deep the fetor of death rising from the corpses of your brothers! Look hard upon the pyres of your parents and children! Squint at the Parthenon and the depletion of its treasures! How dare you take ownership of such miseries, rather than acknowledging the parties – no, the singular man – responsible?

"At a minimum, this assembly must strip Pericles of his seat in the Strategeion. At a minimum, he must be fined, in recognition of the contagion his misguided strategy has wrought upon your families. If this assembly fails to assign responsibility, to extract justice and recompense for the torment brought upon the state by his ineptitude...then the Athens you fight for is already lost."

The crowd was driven to mania, shouting obscenities and cursing the house of Pericles. Phormio tried his best to quell the uproar, to no avail. After several minutes of barely controlled chaos, a chastened Pericles took the platform. He waited in silence for the people to settle and commotion to die down.

Hippocrates whispered to Phormio, "I've never seen Greeks worked up to a frenzy like this. Do you think he can talk the crowd down from it?"

"I certainly hope so," said Phormio, both lament and anxiety in his voice.

"I was not unprepared for the indignation of which I have been the object, as I know its causes," said Pericles. "And yet if you are angry with me, it is with one who, as I believe, is second to no man either in knowledge of the proper policy, or in the ability to expound it, and who is moreover not only a patriot but an honest one. I am the same man and do not alter. It is you who change, since in fact you took my advice while unhurt, and waited for misfortune to repent of it. The apparent error of my policy lies in the infirmity of your resolution, since the suffering that it entails is being felt by every one among you, while its advantage is still remote and obscure to all. Your mind is too much depressed to persevere in your resolves...the spirit quails.

"The plague has certainly been an emergency. Born, however, as you are, citizens of a great state, and brought up, as you have been, with habits equal to your birth, you should be ready to face the greatest disasters. Cease then to grieve for your private afflictions, and address yourselves instead to the safety of the commonwealth. You may think it is a great privation to lose the use of your land and houses. You should know too that liberty preserved by your efforts will easily recover for us what we have lost.

"You must not be seduced by citizens like these or angry with me – who, if I voted for war, only did as you did yourselves. The plague that has come upon us is the only point at which our calculation has been at fault. If your country has the greatest name in all the world, it is because she never bent before disaster.

"Hatred at the moment has fallen to all who have aspired to rule others. But hatred also is short-lived. That which makes the glory of the future remains forever unforgotten. Make your decision, then."

Hippocrates fought the urge to hang his head. "For a man gifted with words, that speech was tone-deaf and callous."

Phormio grunted. "Follow through on your plans to treat the sick, Asklepiad. Leave the run of Athens to its leaders." He remained stone-faced as Cleon led the assembly in a vote to oust Pericles from the *strategoi* and levy a severe fine against the First Citizen's personal wealth.

"What happens now?" said Hippocrates.

"Nothing good," said Phormio, and left the Pnyx in stoic silence.

Despite his angst over Pericles' fall from power, Phormio proved a strong motivator for the troops, and the response proceeded quicker than Hippocrates had expected. Athens was still oppressively overcrowded, and new cases of plague arose daily. But an intensive effort to rehabilitate the Long Walls corridor was initiated, filling in cesspits and cleansing the walkway of filth and rot. Within days of the emergent and fateful assembly, foot traffic resumed between Athens and Piraeus.

The neglected dead were sought out, discovered, and cremated in short order, with their remains interred at public expense. As for the abandoned wretched behind city walls, the public archivists worked to connect the widows and orphans with distant relations, guided by kinship and religious ties.

Thousands of mostly healthy refugees were dispersed into less crowded neighborhoods by the ports of Piraeus. When news arrived that the Spartan army, fearing the pestilence, was avoiding further incursions into Attica, soldiers escorted rural families back to their farmsteads. In the spirit of civic duty, Athens' aristocrats provided the farmers with slave labor to reclaim arable land.

The bonfires cleansed the air of pollution and the stench of death, and protection of the fresh water supply brought about a noticeable drop in fatal intestinal bleeding among the sick and disabled. It was a painful, exhausting few weeks to implement the recovery plan. But Athens looked poised to reclaim its glory, and Hippocrates could finally rest soundly again.

TWENTY-THREE

"No! Gods, no!"

Hippocrates was in a dead sleep when the piercing cry jolted him awake well before the dawn. He sat up, calm but disoriented to time and place. The shuffling of feet and clanging of lanterns brought his senses into focus. That came from inside the house, he thought, but where?

"Hippocrates! Help!"

"Democritus?" shouted Hippocrates. "Where are you?" The elder Gorgias let out an annoyed grunt but fell back into deep snoring.

"We're in the woman's quarter!"

Hippocrates blinked his head clear. A slave, lantern in hand, ushered him to the women's bedroom. Thaïs stood by

Euthalia's bedside, the linens soaked through with blood, while a frantic Democritus paced around the room.

"Gods!" said Hippocrates. "What's happened?"

"It's the plague!" said Democritus. "Just like you've told us! She's purging blood!" Democritus fell into Hippocrates' arms, weeping. "You've got to save her! You've got to save her!"

Euthalia, gray and sweaty, tried to sit up. Thaïs stacked cushions for support, but to no avail. The *hetaera* collapsed back on the bed, rapid and shallow of breath. Hippocrates motioned for a slave to fetch water and moist towels, then politely asked all but his companions to vacate the room.

"Do you have the strength to talk?" said Hippocrates.

"Barely, Asklepiad," said Euthalia, still with eyes closed. "And apologies for breaking up your beauty sleep."

"Disease cares little about the hour of the day," said Hippocrates. "Tell me what happened."

"She's barely alert!" said Democritus. "Can we not just light a small bonfire to clean the air? Isn't that what you're doing across the city?"

"That's not how it works," said Hippocrates, "and every patient is different, even if the affliction is the same."

"It's okay, Democritus," said Euthalia. "He needs to do his job." Democritus harrumphed and resumed his nervous pacing.

Hippocrates sat down and gave Euthalia a cup of water. "Tell me what's happened. Take all the time you need."

Euthalia sat up, took a few sips, then lay back down. "My sleep was restful, despite an upset stomach. A wave of nausea came over me, then intense cramps, and I felt the hot gush of blood from my insides."

"I've been away from the house," said Hippocrates. "Have you been in any public buildings or temples for the sick?"

"No," said Euthalia. I've barely left the house.

"Had you felt any symptoms before today?"

"My sense of taste has been off, otherwise no."

"Any fevers? Pain or foul taste in the mouth? Coughing or retching?"

"No, Asklepiad."

Hippocrates stroked his beard in thought. "Democritus, I need to examine Euthalia at the source of the bleeding. While I can't force you to leave, I've found over the years that husbands and fathers are rarely comfortable around a woman's privy parts during an examination. Do you mind?"

Democritus grumbled and left the room without a word, too stricken with panic to debate his physician friend. Hippocrates grabbed a lantern and held it up under the bloodied bedsheets. He spied a small mixture of tissue and clot in a large pool of fresh blood. As he suspected, the blood tracked down Euthalia's thigh from her vagina.

"Thaïs, can I ask you to mix some *hydromel*?" said Hippocrates. "Use the usual ratio of water to honey. And do ask the house servants to gather what clean linens they have. I'll dispose of these bloody ones and see that they're burned. Come the daytime Democritus will reimburse the household." Thaïs nodded and bowed out of the room.

Hippocrates sat back down on the bed and reached for Euthalia's hand, holding it softly. "Did he know?"

Euthalia's eyes watered. "No," she said meekly, squeezing the physician's hand. "I'd miscarried years ago, while still a girl. An older man...he..."

"I understand," said Hippocrates, his own eyes welling up.

"I never conceived a child after that day. I assumed I was barren, which made it...made it easier to get into my line of work. But Democritus was different. He wasn't just another client, another transaction."

"No. He's a good man, and he loves you deeply."

Euthalia sobbed. "He was so good to me. So kind, so generous."

"Look, whatever comes of this, I'm sorry for every petty insult. You were never anything but a perfect houseguest, and the best thing to ever happen to Democritus."

"This is the end for me, isn't it?"

"I'll do what I can, but you've lost a lot of blood. You're also still oozing, so there's likely more yet to pass."

"I must look awful. The one thing I could always count on..."

"Oh, please. On your worst day, you're the most striking, cultured woman I've ever met. And I was proud to see you on the arm of my oldest friend."

"Whether I live or die, promise me you won't tell him. Losing me is one thing. If he knows he's lost a child as well..."

"I won't." The two held hands and cried as the first rays of dawn broke up the darkness.

Moments later, Thaïs returned with a stack of fresh bedlinens and Democritus in tow. The distraught philosopher pulled Hippocrates aside. "Tell me everything, Asklepiad," said Democritus. "I'm not a child."

"It's just as you feared," said Hippocrates. "The pestilence has her." And her secret was safe.

TWENTY-FOUR

Hippocrates hurried as best he could to check on the infirmaries within a square mile of the *agora*. Within days of his early springtime arrival in Athens, he'd identified which of his student recruits had a knack for the Art, and which ones were slow to catch on. The quickest and most capable students were put in charge of the outlying sites, particularly in Piraeus, while those in need of more guidance Hippocrates kept close by. It worked as well as could be expected, given the onslaught of sick Athenians and limited space and supplies. On most days Hippocrates relished the time to teach, to reinforce the value of observation and the duty to share discoveries. This day was different, however, as his visits were short and his directions terse.

Euthalia took her last breaths an hour after dawn, casting a pall over the household. Thaïs, who'd developed a big-sisterly admiration for the cultured *hetaera*, volunteered to prepare the body for burial, performing the rites of cleaning and dressing Euthalia in a proper gown. Democritus was distraught, in hysterics even, but refused both wine and Hippocrates' offer of an herbal sedative.

"I need to feel the pain," a sobbing Democritus had told his close friend. "Does that make sense?"

"It does," Hippocrates had said. "We'll all feel the pain for some time to come."

"Will you be giving the eulogy?"

"No. I haven't the time to prepare one, with my duties to the ill and the suffering taking precedence. I spoke with Gorgias, who's both humbled and honored to speak."

"You're going to let the woman I loved be sent to the afterlife with flowery tricks of the tongue?!?"

"I understand your anger, Democritus, but have faith in the love and good sense of your friends."

Polus helped arrange for a funeral plot in Kerameikos and offered his household servants to take part in the procession and mourning. Unlike the grand public funerals, a single funeral, even for the wealthy, was an intimate family affair. Democritus tore at his hair and garments for most of the walk, and Hippocrates clutched a crying Thaïs at his side, providing comfort as a father might to his daughter. Polus, as head of the house, led the hymns and libations as impromptu priest. After Euthalia was interred and offerings were laid at the graveside, Gorgias stepped forward.

"A poem by Sappho," said Gorgias.

"When I have departed,
Say but this behind me,
'Love was all her wisdom,
All her care.
Well she kept love's secret,
Dared and never faltered,
Laughed and never doubted
Love would win.
Let the world's rough triumph
Trample by above her,
She is safe forever from all harm.
In a land that knows not
Bitterness nor sorrow,
She has found out all
Of truth at last.'

"I'm so sorry, old friend." A tearful Gorgias embraced Democritus, who dropped to his knees sobbing.

Polus' house fell all but silent through the evening, with servants' murmurs the only ambient sounds. Gorgias and Polus had gone elsewhere for the supper meal, while Democritus, disconsolate with grief, picked at some fruits and sought solace in the home's courtyard.

Hippocrates tried burying himself in work, grazing on snacks while rereading his journals from the early days of the plague, but found concentrating impossible. By the dim light of an oil lamp, his mind wandered through all he had seen in the past year. Battlefield injuries, fungating wounds, hemorrhagic ulcers, barbarism in the streets...and death. Thousands and thousands of his fellow Greeks – Athenians and otherwise – dying so rapidly and in numbers so vast, the scale of the tragedy was abstract. And despite all his efforts, all the knowledge of his predecessors and the insights of his students, Hippocrates was powerless to do anything but mitigate slightly the greatest disaster he'd ever known.

And the effort had left him spent. Not that he'd ever been a heavy sleeper, but it had been months since he'd woken fresh for the day. Is that why my eye won't stop twitching, he wondered in exasperation.

A tap on the shoulder startled him. "Yes? What!" He swerved around.

"I'm sorry to bother you, Asklepiad," said Thaïs. "I noticed your lantern flickering. I know your habit of working into the night, so I'm only here to refill it with oil. I'll be quick and leave you to your work."

"Oh, yes, thank you," said Hippocrates.

He watched Thaïs take extra care at her task, checking and double-checking that she hadn't spilled any oil. Work at the infirmaries had been so frenetic, he'd barely noticed that Thaïs was coming into her figure as a young woman. As she stood up and pulled her hair back, he stared at the outline of her figure in the lamplight. How long had he been away from Theokleia? Since he'd felt the warmth of woman's body next to his own? Since he'd tended to his own needs?

Hippocrates stood and grasped Thaïs gently by the upper arms. "Thank you for everything, Thaïs." His fingers stroked her shoulders. Her skin was flawless, silken. Thaïs froze. "What's the matter?"

"Nothing, my Lord."

He continued to caress her in silence. "You're hardly breathing. And you've gone tense."

"Nothing is wrong, my Lord."

Hippocrates flashed back to the first night he'd met Thaïs, when she still carried the slave name Thratta, dressed in shabby, tattered rags, standing over the dying body of...

Hippocrates yanked his hands away at once. "I'm so sorry," said Hippocrates. "You're...you're part of my family. That was inappropriate. I don't know what came over me."

But he did know. A year drowning in pain and in war, agony and mourning, desperation and death. It had eaten away at him, day by day and hour by hour. In the city that embodied the apex of Greek glory and splendor, he'd found only tragedy and grief.

Hippocrates fell to his knees, first weeping then bawling, hugging the legs of his servant-girl like a frightened toddler clinging to his mother. Thaïs simply stood over him, stroking his head patiently into the night, until the wave of anguish ebbed.

TWENTY-FIVE

As they emerged from under the shade of the Propylaea gateway, Hippocrates and Democritus blinked away the glare off the *Athena Promachos*. The dazzling bronze colossus greeted all visitors and worshippers on the rocky Acropolis. Forged in a martial pose, with a shield held straight on the left arm and a spear brandished in the right, the statue was a towering monument to the military prowess of Athens and her patron goddess.

"What do you think?" said Democritus. "Fifteen cubits?" He'd spent days in mourning, confining himself to the house and rejecting the company of even his oldest friend.

"Closer to twenty, I think," said Hippocrates, "not including the pedestal. Magnificent."

"They say on a cloudless day, you can see the glint of the spear all the way from the southwest tip of Attica, beyond the Lavrion mines," said Democritus. "Personally, I prefer the *Athena Parthenos*, the sculptor's masterwork. The ivory and gold, the intricacy of the relief images on the shield...and the eyes, cunning and alluring all at once. It's a pity they keep her locked up inside in the Parthenon."

"Too delicate to leave exposed in the winter, I'd think. And if the war drags on, they'll need to melt the gold to pay for troops and arms. The statue might not look right stripped of its gilding."

They turned south, strolling along the long edge of that other symbol of Athenian dominance, the Parthenon, taking inventory of the relief sculptures wrapped around the metopes under the pitched roof.

"Come on, Asklepiad," said Democritus. "What are we doing here? You didn't drag me up to the Acropolis, lovely as it is, to admire statues."

"My, you're impatient when you're sober," said Hippocrates.

"It's why I avoid it whenever possible."

"Come to the ledge with me."

"Why? Were you thinking we should leap to our doom? I prefer we do it in a bronze chariot, riding it over the cliff like Theseus and Lykos."

"Theseus and who that did what?!? What legend is that?"

"I made it up. Look, I'm neither in the mood for a long speech nor a suicide pact, so can we go back—"

"Just come to the ledge and look down." The south face of the Acropolis plateau was dangerously steep, much like the northern face. Apart from the massive retaining wall fortification, the only noteworthy sight was the Theatre of Dionysus and its accompanying Odeon, directly south of the Parthenon's east entrance.

"What am I looking at?" said Democritus.

"Next to the Theatre," said Hippocrates, pointing down. "That's the site. The future infirmary. My student Telemachos fancies himself a future priest of Asklepios, overseeing a temple to the god of the Art. From the suffering and death wrought by the plague, healing and hope."

"That's amazing! Who would have thought a backwater islander could conquer Athens without a single toss of a spear?"

"I'm hardly a conqueror."

"You won their hearts and minds, Asklepiad. And while many thousands have died, many thousands that were otherwise doomed will now survive. You fought off the deadliest curse of this gods-cursed war...no small feat."

"But I couldn't fight off what mattered most to you. I'm sorry I couldn't save her, Democritus."

Democritus welled up with tears. "I know you did what you could. Tell me...you've seen countless families torn apart by pestilence and disease and untimely death, husbands burying their wives, parents burying their children...does the pain ever subside? Do we ever forget and move on?"

"Some do, or at least profess to. Except for those wretches in truly miserable marriages, though, I don't believe them. I've seen grief and pain denied among some barbarian cultures, but it's unhealthy. Holding back such powerful emotions causes a buildup of black bile. It poisons the mind and the body."

"Melancholy?"

"Melancholy."

"I loved her, Hippocrates. You always joked that I had to pay her, but—"

"It was all in jest. I apologized in her final hours and told her what I really thought of her. She was a stunningly beautiful, cultured woman, and she made you happy. It's also time I shared a secret she was keeping from you."

"What secret? She kept secrets from me?"

"She did, and it was this: you were never a paying client to her. She adored you with every fiber of her being."

Democritus fell to the ground, wailing. Hippocrates kneeled, crying alongside his friend. Some moments later, they rose and toured the Acropolis in silent reflection. They crossed the foundations of temples burned down by the

Persians. They eavesdropped on the hymns of maidens practicing a dance for the next great festival. And they traced the shadow of the sacred olive tree, descendant of the one gifted by Athena in her victory over Poseidon for patronage of the city.

Their meandering was interrupted by a slave they recognized from Polus' home darting from out of the Propylaea, flanked by two of Athens' sentry archers. "Hippocrates! Hippocrates!" Hippocrates waved him over. "I'm sorry, sir. The sentries are here to escort you to the Areopagus."

"Isn't that the court that tries homicide cases? Am I under arrest?" said Hippocrates.

"You've been summoned to prepare expert testimony," said one of the sentries, "for the trial of Onesimos the slave trader."

It struck outsiders as odd that the most ancient and revered court in Greece was little more than an open-air mound of rock. But the Areopagus, the hill due west of the Acropolis, and the council that met atop it, had its origins in legend. It was said that on that very hill, Ares himself stood trial for the murder of Halirrhothius, son of Poseidon.

Whatever the truth behind the old stories, the Areopagus had fallen out of favor as a high council after the Persian wars, its jurisdiction and authority stripped in accordance with the growth and maturation of the democracy. The council's aristocratic character spent half a century as the flashpoint of conflict between Athens' conservatives and populist democrats, radicals led by Pericles and his political mentors. But as a gathering of four hundred former Archons of the *polis*, the Athenians could still point to the Areopagus as a just and venerable court of law, in particular for trying perpetrators of the gravest crimes. The sophistry and rhetorical tricks that so readily swayed the popular juries were of no use before the staid and educated nobles of the Areopagus.

Onesimus stood expressionless, shackled in iron, as the King Archon read the charges aloud. "Onesimus, son of Arkadios, of the *polis* Eretria, you are charged as a *metic*, a resident alien of Athens, for the crime of murder. The Eponymous Archon Apollodoros will present evidence on behalf of the state."

Just pour the hemlock and be done with it, thought Onesimos. Letter after letter from the survivors read aloud, describing the horror of watching a child die in his own bloody vomit, or hearing a wife scream in torture from visceral pain, or smelling the stench of a dead parent rotting in the midday sun. Then the statement of that gods-cursed physician...the Archon droning on and on, regurgitating medical nonsense he barely understood. Oh, yes, rich old

Athenian jurors, the foreigner's slaves are the source of the plague, and by the grace of that physician's genius the city would rise again.

What could he possibly say to save his own skin? Nobody had his back. If he brought up Kenamon, the jurors would laugh. A slave-trading warlord from the wastelands beyond Egypt...even if they could find him, his word was as credible as ox shit. As for Diokles? How much did he still owe Onesimos for the last bunch? No better way to get out of debt than to see your creditor dispatched to Hades. Kushah? Slave testimony was only valid under torture, and the man barely knew ten words of Greek. Sweet-talk his way out of this himself? These old farts were schooled in all the tricks, and who knows how many of them lost family and fortune in the plague.

So his life was forfeit, that much was for certain. The only question was how. Hemlock was the simplest, but it was a cup of poison in a jail – hardly a way to satisfy the crowd's lust for vengeance. Beheading or hanging could whip the mob into a frenzy, but they were customs of the barbarians. The Egyptians had a storied history of burning their criminals alive...

"Onesimos!" said the presiding King Archon. "You have heard the charges and evidence against you. We will set the waterclock and you may speak in your own defence."

"Athens," said Onesimos, "You started a war. You needed labor, I sold it to you. Did I know the slaves were sick? What if I did? I'm neither a priest nor a physician. I don't know why people get sick, how sickness spreads, nor how to cure it. I'm a merchant, not a medic or a murderer.

"If killing me will provide you a measure of comfort, then end this boring proceeding and get it over with. Flitting about the afterlife alongside your loved ones can't be any more painful than listening to your misdirected rage.

"And it is misdirected. As I said, I just brought your slaves from one place to the next. You should ask yourselves what created the market for slave labor in the first place. Yes, Athens, I refer to your precious empire and glorious war. Is there really a difference if your loved ones are butchered in the sack of a city, rather than dead by the scourge of a plague? If your women are widowed by sickness, or widowed by the tip of a spear?

"So for all your monuments and temples, and the lofty rhetoric of your statesmen and philosophers, you invited this death upon yourselves. Rather than punish me, a passive courier of the pestilence, you should lay blame at what the gods have warned against since time immemorial: your own hubris, Athens, and the empire and war that followed it."

The vote was swift and unanimous, the judgement preordained.

"Onesimos, son of Arkadios," said the King Archon, "this council finds you guilty of murder, causing death on a scale not seen since the war with Persia. Do you have anything to say before your sentence is handed down?"

"Sure. Can I have ten minutes with a whore before you hand me the poison?" said Onesimos.

"I'm afraid poison is too swift an end for one so vile as you," said the King Archon, "and your spirit will have a much harder time finding its way to the afterlife. Guards, are you familiar with the limestone gully by the northern slope of the Acropolis?" The sentries nodded. "Please see that jugs of oil are poured down its walls to ensure they can't be scaled. Then throw this wretch into the gully, with his shackles still on. Set fire to the corpse once it starts to smell."

The sun was nearly set by the time the proceedings came to an end. One by one, the aristocrats of the council came to thank and embrace Hippocrates for his testimony and service to Athens. It was nightfall by the time the physician was through it all. He was escorted off the Areopagus hill, where he was greeted by Democritus.

"So, is that Athenian justice slow enough for you?"

"At least it was served," said Hippocrates. "Now, my friend, I could really use a cup of wine...or six."

"Ha! Won't that leave you grouchy and non-functional to treat patients in the morning?" said Democritus.

"I won't be at the temple tomorrow."

"Was the sun too bright atop that rock? You're showing signs of madness. Two days in a row without working?"

"I didn't say I wouldn't be working. I just have something more pressing to do tomorrow than teach my increasingly capable students."

"What's that?"

"It's time I addressed the cause of this plague at its root."

TWENTY-SIX

Hippocrates was accustomed to calling on the sick in their homes, but social visits were never his strong suit. Part of the problem was his family's wealth and noble status on Kos. His circle of friends growing up was as close-knit as it was affluent. Beyond that, though, practicing the Art meant that most of his personal encounters were between physician and patient, rather than friend to friend. It was an exchange that demanded both his learned opinion and a measure of aloofness, a distance that flowed naturally from the need to stay objective. A clothing merchant or cobbler could be as cold or engaging as he wished – the transaction with his customer didn't turn on the warmth of his character. Medicine was very different, at least to Hippocrates.

Then again, this was no ordinary social call, but a visit to the home of Pericles himself, the most dominant figure in Athenian life for a generation. The man who reformed the democracy, strengthened the empire, spearheaded the rebuilding of the Parthenon...now stripped of his station by power-hungry demagogues. It was the Great Democracy in action, for better or worse.

And yet, it was Pericles' leadership that drove Athens to war, that stuffed the city walls with countryside refugees, laying the groundwork for a pestilence that wrought horror and death on a vast scale. Stripped of power or not, would he own up to his failings? What would Hippocrates say to the great man, one way or the other?

A servant answered Hippocrates' knock, but bid him wait before entering. So far as could be judged from the doorway, Pericles' home was less opulent than those of other Athenian nobles. It wasn't from lack of money. Pericles was head of the Alcmaeonids, a dynasty of Greek nobles that dated back centuries. The moderate décor was rather a reflection of the man's reputed manner and temperament, of class rather than ostentation.

"The famous Hippocrates! Do come in." Hippocrates was stunned to be invited inside not by a servant, but a woman of unparalleled exotic beauty. Her face was flawless in contour, with neither a wrinkle nor blemish to be seen. Her lips were a lustrous red, glowing outward from her deep olive skin. And her gaze was both warm and penetrating, her eyes curious but full of insight.

Aspasia of Miletus, consort of Pericles.

"You must be the famous Aspasia," said Hippocrates. "I've heard many things about you, but none that do justice to your beauty."

"Do I dare ask what else you've heard?" said Aspasia. "Wait, let me guess. I'm a base whore, I run a brothel, I write all of Pericles' speeches, I instigated two wars, including the present one with Sparta, I'm as jealous as Hera, I'm as ruinous to men as Helen of Troy...did I miss anything?"

"I'm no politician and don't put stock in political vitriol," said Hippocrates. "I've simply heard many speak of your glamour, your cultured nature, and the unassuming warmth of your home."

"You know how to flatter, Hippocrates. A difficult art for us foreigners to master, no?"

"There is room in my life for only one art – the Art – and it will never be mastered by any one man. Commending your beauty and grace is merely stating the obvious."

"Okay, enough with the adulation. How can I help you?"

"I beg permission, Aspasia, to speak with your husband Pericles."

"With regards to what, if I might ask?"

Hippocrates was surprised at Aspasia's assertiveness, and stood mouth agape in silence.

"I assume you're confused as to what woman would question the intention of a male visitor to her home," said Aspasia, "in particular a visitor of such great reputation as yourself."

Hippocrates remained stunned, unsure of how to respond.

"I know. You've come to lay blame at the feet of my husband, to drown him in the cisterns of blood that flowed from the plague you ascribe entirely to him. Do you think him so bereft of conscience or shame? Or immune to the venom of his rivals and countrymen?

"If you must speak with Pericles, he's down the hall in the *andron*, drafting a letter to the leadership of the assembly. What letter, you wonder? Could he be so pathetic that he would beg clemency for the hefty fines laid on his estate?

"To answer the question before you pose it, no. While the hacks and demagogues plotted their intrigues, Pericles remained at the bedsides of Paralus and Xanthippus – his only legitimate sons by his harpy of a first wife. Both now lie dead and interred from the plague. Since Athenian law dictates that only a child born to two Athenians is eligible for citizenship, he must now beg – beg! – the assembly to grant the franchise to my son, Pericles the Younger, his only surviving child."

"Pericles gave his own name to a child by his *hetaera*?" said Hippocrates.

"He's been my lover and companion since before he bid the Acropolis rebuilt," said Aspasia. "I am no mere whore to the man."

"No, you aren't. He's blessed by the gods to have you."

Aspasia watched sternly as Hippocrates tiptoed past her to the *andron*. With his back to doorway, Pericles sat at a table, etching his thoughts into a clay tablet, tears streaming down his cheeks. Seemingly oblivious to the visiting physician, Pericles cried out in anguish, smashing tablet after tablet on the ground in frustration and disgust. The greatest orator of his day, distraught and at a loss for words.

Hippocrates watched the scene quietly, more unsure than he'd been all morning. What could he say to any man, never mind a deposed political leader, that had lost two sons ignobly, begging for the legitimacy of a third? A man of advancing age, staring down the end of a line that traced its origins to the crew of the *Argo*? Would the scorn of a physician half the man's age matter?

"I know you're there, Asklepiad," sighed Pericles with back still turned. "Do come in." The elder statesman stood to face his guest. His face was longer and features more angular than those of the younger Hippocrates, but he looked weathered and worn, his godlike aura faded.

Hippocrates found a couch opposite Pericles but stayed upright and stiff. "You have a beautiful home, General." A servant came through offering breadcakes and fruits, but both men waved her away.

"Your memory is short, Asklepiad," said Pericles. "I'm not a member of the *strategoi* anymore. But I can echo the sentiments of my former colleagues. Athens owes you an incalculable debt."

"I did no more than my duty," said Hippocrates. "But thank you."

"Now surely the greatest physician in all of Greece has better things to do than collect more accolades from politicians. What brings you here?"

"Your speech to the assembly, some days ago."

"Not one of my better orations, improvised as it was. What of it?"

"It was callous and defensive, an attempt to deflect blame for your misguided strategy in a misbegotten war."

Pericles froze for an instant, taken aback. "That's one interpretation, and I suppose not an unfair one. Seeing the people swayed so violently against me after so many years of heeding my counsel was a painful blow to bear. But decades in public life have inured me to outbursts of hatred."

"How you felt after being ousted by the people is not my concern."

"No? Have you come to try and correct me, then? To demand that I address the assembly again, take responsibility for the plague, and beg their forgiveness? Are you here to put words in my mouth, like one of your speechwriter friends might do for an illiterate cobbler on trial?"

"No, Pericles, I'm here to learn *why*. Why you crowded the country people into the town in the heat of the summer weather, in small tenements and stifling hovels, tied to a lazy course of life within doors...to keep them pent up like cattle, overrun with infection from one another, affording them neither shift of quarters nor any refreshment."

"There was one principle, Asklepiad, which I held to through everything, and that is the principle of no concession to the Spartans. If we gave way, we would instantly have to meet some greater demand, as having been frightened into obedience in the first instance. All claims from an adversary, be they great or be they small, have only one meaning, and that is slavery.

"Bringing the populace behind the walls was the safest course of action I saw in service of that singular principle. Counsel was demanded of me, and I put it to those who allowed themselves to be persuaded...to support the national resolves, even in the case of setbacks."

Hippocrates rose, enraged. "And what of the plague?!? You would dismiss the lives of thousands that died as a 'setback'? And what of the farmers' fields and orchards put to the torch? What do you say to the widows and orphans, to the childless parents, that watched their families and friends bleed, wither, and rot, all in the name of your singular 'principle'? And apparently, in the name of your stubborn pride?"

Pericles stood too, staring down the upstart physician "Sometimes the course of things is as arbitrary as the plans of man. The spirit which inspires men while they are being persuaded to make war is not always retained in action. As circumstances change, resolutions change."

"But not the resolve of Olympian Pericles."

"With the glory and freedom of Athens at stake? No." A moment of silence passed between the two. "Is there anything else I might help you with, Asklepiad? I have work to return to."

"No," said Hippocrates in disgust and resignation, taking his leave.

History would pass judgement on Pericles, that much was certain. His name would be synonymous with either the glorious monuments of Athens, the downfall of her empire, or perhaps both. But the man's own concerns now lay with what little remained of his family, the fate of his name and the shreds that remained of his pride. Short of ending Pericles' life, there was nothing Hippocrates could do to inflict more suffering upon the man. Nor were there any words that might make the man embrace the consecration of life so central to the Art. It's mercy, thought Hippocrates, only compassion and mercy that remain.

Hippocrates strode towards the front door. "I thank you for your hospitality, Aspasia," he said, "and your insights into your husband's affairs."

"I don't understand, Asklepiad," said Aspasia. "I heard raised voices. What did you talk about?"

"He was busy and asked not to be interrupted," said Hippocrates, "I didn't hear at first, which might explain the raised voices you heard. I left him to his writing. Could I offer one comment before taking my leave?"

"Talk."

"When he goes before the assembly to plead for your son's legitimacy, some of his political enemies might look to blame the plague on him. The worst of the demagogues might be extreme enough to suggest that the plague was divine punishment for Pericles' hubris, the death of his older sons somehow deserved. As the one most qualified to comment on the nature of the plague and its causes, please feel free to call on my testimony to refute such nonsense in support of Pericles' application."

A tearful Aspasia kissed Hippocrates on the cheek. "Thank you, Hippocrates."

TWENTY-SEVEN

The sunlight beaming down on Kerameikos amid a calm breeze belied the somber nature of the day and equally somber mood among the nobles of Athens.

"I can't believe they gave him the honors," said Thucydides.

"I don't see you taking notes," said Democritus. "You're not intending to preserve the speech as 'a gift for all time'?"

"The man's words hardly constitute a gift," said Thucydides.

"My last bowel movement constitutes a greater gift than this man's words," said Aristophanes.

In a stunning turn of events, the Athenian assembly had asked its new and self-appointed leader Cleon to deliver the oration that closed the winter's public funeral for the wartime fallen. Once the autumnal equinox passed, so had the brunt of the plague, and Spartan incursions into the Attic countryside stopped as well. With most casualties of the plague cremated or interred, the city saw its many thousands of refugees return to their rural homesteads to repair their homes and sow fresh crops. In total, a third of the population fell prey to the pestilence, a wake of devastation unmatched by even the bloodiest battles in Greek history.

Cleon staggered forward through the crowd of mourners to the cheers of his ardent supporters.

"Is he drunk?" said Hippocrates. "Please tell me he had the sense not to drink himself into a stupor for a public funeral."

"On the contrary, Asklepiad," said Aristophanes. "He's the leader of the assembly now. He has to set an example for the rank-and-file."

Cleon pounded his chest and held a fist in the air to hush the crowd. "All of us know that public service is a cruel life. We Athenians dedicate our lives to the glory of this *polis*, and honor those that have died in service of that glory, but it remains a cruel life. As a man of strong views, even unpopular views, no man understands that cruelty more than me. And yet until now Athens has been led into war by those who would deny that selfsame cruel reality, that would dismiss the demands for sacrifice, and advocate that rancor has no place in our hearts.

"We stand today to celebrate the glorious deaths of these men, the heroes of Athens that stared down the cruel truth of public service and scoffed. These men embraced the hatred your old leaders called dangerous, and used that hatred to vanquish our enemies, both on the battlefield plains and on the high seas. These men saw the cruel life of public service not as a curse but a gift of the gods, to wield as a hammer against our enemies, and an aegis against a life devoid of significance.

"So, my fellow Athenians, mend the clothes on your back torn in grief, tidy the hairs not ripped from your scalps, and dry the eyes rubbed red from tears, for you have no cause to mourn or despair. Today, I am your voice in the face of loss and failed leadership. I am your voice in the quest for victory and vengeance. We spit in the face of the cruelty of public service, and speak defiantly, 'Athens will not merely endure, but reign supreme!'" With that, Cleon shooed away the mourners and went about embracing his friends and backers.

"That was...something," said Democritus.

"I look forward to combat operations instead of listening to this man lead the assembly," said Thucydides.

"I owe General Kleitos an apology for insulting his brusque behavior," said Gorgias. "He's an exemplar of etiquette and guardian of grace next to this besotted brute and his vacuous vainglory."

"For once I agree with you wholeheartedly, Gorgias," said Hippocrates. "That was painful."

"I disagree," said Aristophanes. "Unpleasant, yes, but it's not like you had to sleep with him. That, I imagine, would be painful. I mean, the chafing alone..."

Hippocrates couldn't help but snicker, despite the pall cast by the funerary procession. "Aristophanes, you entertain me to no end. Come by the home of Polus this afternoon. I have a matter of some importance to discuss with you."

"Whatever it is, it's not my doing," said Aristophanes.

"I promise only good news," said Hippocrates, "a commodity in short supply these days."

"You're going back to Abdera?" said Hippocrates.

"No," said Democritus, sorting his belongings into parcels and chugging a cupful of wine. "I've always fancied spending time in Egypt, based on your stories. And who knows where my travels might take me from there? Getting away from a bloody civil war will give me time and space to write. I've at least a dozen treatises to write on this, that, and the other, and plenty of coin to buy safe passage."

"I hope you find cheer," said Hippocrates. "You're too jolly to spend your days moping around the Mediterranean."

"I hope so too," said Democritus with a winsome smile.

"And you, Gorgias?"

"I have some affairs to see to back home at Leontini," said Gorgias, "but anticipate a return to Athens in the near future. I've built quite a following here, you know."

"Clearly humility and rhetoric are not overly compatible as teachable subjects," murmured Democritus.

"I beg your pardon?" said Gorgias.

"Nothing, Teacher," said Hippocrates and Democritus in unison.

"And you, Asklepiad?" said Gorgias.

"I'll stay in Athens through winter to prepare my cadre of students for independent practice," said Hippocrates, "but then I'd like to return home to Kos. Theokleia's given birth to another boy, Draco. She's no doubt desperate for my company. I could also use the time to write. I've amassed a good deal of reflections that need to be recorded. Athens is too busy to afford me the time. And like you, Democritus, I'll appreciate being away from the war."

A servant rushed into the *andron*. "Hippocrates? I'm sorry for the interruption, but the *ephebe* Aristophanes has arrived as per your summons."

"Oh good," said Hippocrates. "Can I bother you to find Thaïs and send her here?"

"As you wish," said the servant, bowing out of the room.

A bewildered Aristophanes exchanged greetings with Hippocrates and his friends, making chit-chat until Thaïs was escorted into the *andron.*

"Perfect, everyone's here," said Hippocrates. "As you all know, my father passed away at a younger age than many of his contemporaries, leaving me as head of the household. Among the many responsibilities now resting upon my shoulders, securing a good marriage for my siblings is perhaps the most important, at least after ensuring the continuity of my father's bloodline.

"You, Aristophanes, remarked some months ago that the skills Thaïs has displayed while maintaining the run of the infirmary would do her well in the run of a household. I also recall the first time we met, when you sought my physician's attention for a grave medical condition that imperiled your ability to serve in the military."

Gorgias whispered to Democritus, "What is he talking about? Didn't the young man have a scratch on his leg? And since when does he have a sister?"

"Just keep it to yourself and I'll explain later, Teacher," said Democritus under his breath. "I think I know what he's up to."

"Despite your...infirmity," said Hippocrates, "you are a young man of obvious character, to say nothing of your noble upbringing. I see an impressive future for you as a playwright of comedies. It is therefore with a great deal of pride I offer you the hand of the last free woman of my father's house – my sister Thaïs – as wife and manager of your household." Hippocrates winked and mouthed a shush at a confused Thaïs.

"I'm sorry...you wish for your sister to become my wife?!?" said Aristophanes.

"Is my name not noble enough?" said Hippocrates.

"Not at all," said Aristophanes. "I'm overwhelmed. Thank you, Asklepiad. But I'm not even finished my term in the *ephebes*. I haven't a clue where I might be dispatched to for combat service. And I have no job or household to speak of."

"About that," said Hippocrates, "there's time to iron out the details, including the size of Thaïs' dowry. More importantly, I've drafted a physician's letter for your commanders. Given your history of swooning, it would be both negligent and dangerous to have you spend any more time in the military and risk harming your fellow hoplites in battle. I'm recommending that for medical reasons, you should be excused from military service this day forward."

"For...swooning?"

"Is that not the problem you came to see me for when I first arrived?" Hippocrates winked. "With regrets, caring for victims of the plague has blurred my memory somewhat."

"Um, no, your memory is impeccable, as would be expected of any notable physician."

"Wonderful. Still, as you belong to a wealthy family, the size of a dowry will matter little to your financial position. I'm therefore placing two conditions on the marriage. First, Thaïs is a free woman from a family of means. You will treat her with the same honor and respect that you would any other woman of noble birth. If you don't, I will rescind my recommendations with regards to your fitness, and you will almost certainly face fines or ostracism for military delinquency."

Aristophanes blushed and smiled at Thaïs. "Neither you nor your sister have cause for concern. What's the other condition?"

"Use your comic gifts to make that overstuffed satyr Cleon and his cronies squirm at each and every performance."

Aristophanes grinned ear to ear. "On that measure I vow to be more dependable than the sunrise. Thank you, great Physician!" He kissed Thaïs on the cheek and bounded away in delight.

Sometime later, Thaïs confronted a lone Hippocrates snacking on fruits and olives. "I'm at a loss for words, Asklepiad."

"More than a year ago I declared you *oiketes*, part of my household," said Hippocrates. "You've served me dutifully and unfailingly. It's time I lived up to my obligations as head of the family."

"But freedom and marriage?!? I'm not worthy of the honor."

"The only thing you aren't worthy of is a life as a slave or a spinster. And I can tell that this Aristophanes, prone as he will be to falling in trouble with politicians, has a good heart and a sharp mind. He'll do well by you. But if for some reason he doesn't, there's plenty of space to enjoy your freedom on Kos."

"Thank you, Hippocrates."

Hippocrates kissed Thaïs on the forehead. "I'll miss you."

TWENTY-EIGHT

As the light of the sunset faded, Hippocrates watched Thessalus blink himself to sleep, his breath not quite in step with his baby brother's. Theokleia crept up behind her husband, kissing his bare shoulder and rubbing a hand through his hair.

"You're starting to go bald," whispered Theokleia. "It makes you look wiser."

"They both have your eyes," said Hippocrates. "I missed them. I missed you."

"How long until duty will whisk you away once more?" said Theokleia.

"Not this year. Come, let's sit and talk over a cup of wine."

"The unflappable Hippocrates, indulging in a drink?

"A year in Athens does strange things to a man's sanity." The couple cuddled on a couch in the courtyard, savoring the air of the night.

A month had passed since Hippocrates returned to Kos, but this was the first night of peace he'd enjoyed. Kleitos had insisted the physician spend a week as a pampered guest, out of gratitude for Hippocrates' surgical attention and a budding close friendship. Both the household and temple accounts needed review, a necessary pain after an absence of almost two years. And Hippocrates held an intense retreat for his students and colleagues, sharing the lessons he'd learned in the response to the plague, and coaching them in surgical techniques he'd honed while in Athens.

"So, noble Asklepiad," said Theokleia, "how will you ever pass the time, without saving thousands from a pestilence, or sewing up legions of wounded soldiers? Surely the belly cramps of Koan housewives and colored phlegm of shepherds won't be enough to sustain a world-travelled man of medicine."

"Teaching, writing, and just thinking," said Hippocrates. "That's all. The simple life...for a while, anyway."

"Thinking about what? All the exotic *hetaerae* you left behind in Athens?

"Me with *hetaerae*? Gods, no! I have battle plans to draw up. Gorgias and I are leading a squadron of hoplites back into

Sarmatia. I plan to capture and impregnate every one-breasted virgin horse-mistress myself. If I don't act, the Minotaur will beat me to it."

"You're not funny."

"And you have nothing to worry about."

"So what will you be...thinking about in all your spare time?"

"It's a funny thing, my Art. Other than battle, there's no other job in which death is just part of the routine. Witness a death, send the body to the grieving family, and move on. The young, the old, the wealthy, the enslaved...nothing but a corpse to hand off once it's taken a last breath. You can go days, even weeks, and it doesn't make you flinch."

"Until it does."

"Until it does. And then all the pain and the grief overwhelm you, as if you're a gull caught by a wave crashing on a cliffside. But just when you think you're doomed, the grief is swept away. A mother nurses her crying newborn, a little girl wakes from a delirium, an athlete returns to his games...life and hope are renewed, by the grace and the duty of the healer's Art."

"That's beautiful."

"So are you, my love." Hippocrates took his wife by the hand, and they made love in the quiet calm of the moonlight.

The next morning, Hippocrates woke and strode to his work table. He took out a blank clay tablet and etching tool, then paused to reflect on the last two years of his work. He thought of the slave-child and his mother, cut down at the campsite near Potidaea. He thought of the wide-eyed enthusiasm of Artemisios, and the diligence of Telemachos in Athens. He thought of Euthalia's secret that he'd take to his grave. He thought of his former slave and protégé Thaïs, and how close he was to violating her in his moment of weakness. He thought of Athens, and the endurance of its spirit in the face of a devastating plague. He thought of the privileges and duties conferred upon him and his brother physicians. He thought of the Art, and its future throughout Greece and beyond. And with all these ideas dashing inside his head, he wrote:

The Oath

I swear by Apollo the Healer, by Asklepios, by Hygieia, by Panacea, and by all the gods and goddesses, that, according to my ability and judgment, I will keep this Oath and this stipulation – to reckon him who taught me this Art equally dear to me as my parents, to share my substance with him, and relieve his necessities if required; to look upon his offspring in the same footing as my own brothers, and to teach them this Art, if they shall wish to learn it, without fee or stipulation; and that by precept, lecture, and every other mode of instruction, I will impart a knowledge of the Art to my own sons, and those of my teachers, and to disciples bound by a stipulation and oath according to the law of medicine, but to none others.

I will follow that system of regimen which, according to my ability and judgement, I consider for the benefit of my patients, and abstain from whatever is deleterious and mischievous. I will give no deadly medicine to any one if asked, nor suggest any such counsel; and in like manner I will not give to a woman a pessary to produce abortion. With purity and with holiness I will pass my life and practice my Art. I will not cut persons laboring under the stone, but will leave this to be done by men who are practitioners of this work.

Into whatever houses I enter, I will go into them for the benefit of the sick, and will abstain from every voluntary act of mischief and corruption; and, further from the seduction of females or males, of freemen and slaves. Whatever, in connection with my professional practice or not, in connection with it, I see or hear, in the life of men, which ought not to be spoken of abroad, I will not divulge, as reckoning that all such should be kept secret.

While I continue to keep this Oath unviolated, may it be granted to me to enjoy life and the practice of the Art, respected by all men, in all times! But should I trespass and violate this Oath, may the reverse be my lot!

AUTHOR'S NOTE

For a man as important to medical history as Hippocrates, it's strange that not much is known for certain about him, or at least not much on which to form a picture of his character. He was born in or around 460 BCE, the son of a physician and possible priest to Asklepios/Asclepius. His home was the island of Kos/Cos in the southeast Aegean Sea, but he traveled extensively around the ancient Mediterranean, meeting his death in Larissa around 370 BCE. He had two sons, Thessalus and Draco, and a son-in-law named Polybus, all of whom grew to become physicians.

Once we look past the vitals – pardon the medical pun – we must, however, celebrate the legacy of Hippocrates on the art of medicine. And though it might sound surprising, I'm not referring to the *Hippocratic Oath* sworn by every new doctor upon graduating medical school. The modern-day vow bears little resemblance to the oath sworn to pagan gods and demi-gods in the lifetime of Hippocrates and the centuries that followed. And while the oldest extant versions include tenets of practice that survive nowadays, such as patient confidentiality and the duty to teach, one also finds language around euthanasia and abortion that medicine has long since – and perhaps unfortunately – deferred to politics to sort out.

No, Hippocrates' greatest gift was the rejection of disease as the work of the gods. For all we associate Classical Greece with great intellectual achievements in mathematics, politics, history, and philosophy, it's easy to forget that it was a country and culture steeped in Bronze Age superstition. Oracles to the gods were routinely consulted before engaging in military conflict, animal sacrifice was ubiquitous, and the modern world would probably view the festival activities as quaint (minus the live sex acts that might have gone on). Before Hippocrates, illness and plague lay firmly in the hands of fickle and vain gods. Human disease could be anything from divine punishment targeted at a single person, to a "friendly fire" incident while the gods engaged in their endless and petty pissing contests.

That Hippocratic principle of rigorous clinical-environmental observation as a replacement for blind dread of the gods is all the more impressive when you realize that the ancient Greeks did not perform human dissection. Anatomy is the most foundational medical science and isn't subject to wacky theories on how the body works: the left heart pumps blood to the organs and tissues via the aorta and returns it via the great veins to the right heart. End of story. Sadly, it means Hippocrates left us with the pseudoscience of humorism as an explanation for disease...a big leap from the whim of the gods, but a far cry from the scientific medicine that's done wonders for human longevity.

If Hippocrates' character is something of an unknown, the collection of writings attributed to him – the *Hippocratic Corpus* – are simply too diverse to be taken as the work of one man. There are the writings we've all heard about, like *Aphorisms* (source of the timeless quote, "Life is short, and Art long."), the *Oath*, and *On Airs, Waters, and Places*. And some of the shorter documents include prescriptive advice on a physician's dress and demeanor, tips that no doubt informed the modern-day stereotype of the kindly, perceptive, sharp-dressed male doctor. But the *Corpus* also includes highly technical guidebooks on fractures, head injuries, and proctology, to name a few. It's impossible to believe that any one physician could amass enough experience to write definitively on all these subjects. Scholars view the *Corpus* as having been written by many men over many decades, if not several centuries. One of the fun parts of writing fiction, though, is that I'm not bound by scholarly opinion. Where I found something in the *Corpus* that was worth adding into the story, I added it. In fact, many of the speeches given by Hippocrates in the story are lifted word-for-word from the *Corpus*, particularly the *Precepts*. If something literally has Hippocrates' name written all over it, who am I to deny him the honor?

Hippocrates would have practiced medicine at the time of the Peloponnesian War between Athens and the Peloponnesian confederacy led by Sparta. Sparta has been caricatured for more than two thousand years as a backwards, martial society. It's a reputation that comes down to us from antiquity in the *Parallel Lives* of Plutarch but endures into the 21st century thanks to the comic book and movie *300*. What we know about Sparta suggests it was both oligarchical and conservative, but hardly a nation of kamikaze berserkers. The war was formally declared in 431 BCE, after the breakdown of a thirty-year peace negotiated fourteen to fifteen years earlier. Though a small-scale war in terms of numbers, even by ancient standards, the Peloponnesian War, like all civil wars, was devastating in both its human and civic consequences.

The most immediate and most deathly consequence of the Peloponnesian War was the Plague of Athens that broke out in 430 BCE. It's estimated that the plague wiped out between a quarter and a third of the population of Athens and its surrounding countryside of Attica. In his *History of the Peloponnesian War*, Thucydides paints a vivid and harrowing description of the plague, both in terms of its clinical features – symptoms, sequelae, mortality – and the breakdown in moral order that followed.

Historians, doctors, and researchers have spent centuries trying to make an accurate diagnosis of the plague, and one comes across many arguments for one virus or bacterium over another in the medical and historical literature. Analysis of human remains recovered from archaeological digs suggests typhus, but that diagnosis is problematic. The bacterium commonly responsible for typhus is endemic to the region, so would show up in lab tests anyways. Moreover, the symptoms of typhus correspond poorly to the description by Thucydides. Ebola, or an Ebola-like illness that has since mutated into something else (even Ebola itself) is also a common suggestion in the medical literature, as are bubonic plague and cholera.

As I note above, fiction provides an author with a creative license free from the strict limits set by scholars. For the purposes of the story, I modeled the plague on cholera in combination with Lassa fever, a viral hemorrhagic fever much like Ebola arising from contact with rodents. Athens lacks the abundant freshwater springs of other ancient cities, notably Rome. When the population of the city swelled with refugees from the countryside during the war, water and sanitation problems would have been unavoidable, fertile ground for the spread of cholera. There's also no medical reason that the plague must have been caused by a single disease, given the conditions in Athens at the time. As Dr. John Hickam's dictum goes, "A man can have as many diseases as he damn well pleases."

It's easy to look back and wonder what Pericles – the larger-than-life political leader of Classical Athens – was thinking when he thought that Athens could maintain such an acute and extreme increase in her population during the "combat season" each summer. Easy to wonder, but not entirely fair. Athens saw large increases in its population each year for the Panathenaea festival, roughly corresponding to the peak of summer in July. And Athens' colonies around the Black Sea provided a steady supply of grains that would keep the population from starving.

Though people without an interest in Classical Studies likely know little about Pericles, he deserves his place as a giant of democratic history alongside Abraham Lincoln and Winston Churchill. It was Pericles that drove then-radical democratic reforms that stripped the aristocracy of power and put it in the hands of the juries and assembly comprised largely of the poor and working class. It was Pericles who directed the fruits of Athens' empire into major public building projects, most notably the monuments atop the Athenian Acropolis. And it was during the life of Pericles that the artistic and intellectual life of Athens flourished. That his career and life would end so ignominiously – Pericles died from the plague in 429 BCE – seems a shame. For that reason, I did what I could not to put words into the mouth of the great man, instead transcribing directly from Thucydides where possible, or paraphrasing when necessary.

But Pericles had no shortage of critics, even in antiquity. Hippocrates' expressed anger at Pericles in chapter 26 is lifted in part from Plutarch's *Life of Pericles*. And for a more contemporary example of Pericles' critics, one need not look further than the great tragedian Sophocles. In fact, the most straightforward interpretation of Sophocles' masterwork *Oedipus Rex* has nothing to do with Sigmund Freud's sexual fantasies, nor metaphysical questions around free will. Rather, the events in *Oedipus Rex* are perhaps best seen as a political indictment of Pericles, albeit a posthumous one. Sophocles presents Oedipus as king over a Thebes ravaged by plague, a plague sent by the gods as punishment for Oedipus' killing of his own father and subsequent ascent to the throne. As *Oedipus Rex* was probably staged in 426 or 425 BCE, after the devastation of the plague had finally abated, it's easy to see how Sophocles – an aristocrat and likely no fan of the democracy – would be inclined to point a finger at Pericles.

This novel tries to imagine what would have happened had Hippocrates been present in Athens at the time of the plague – how he would have perceived it, responded to it, and dealt with its impact personally. The 2nd century CE gynecologist Soranus wrote a biography of Hippocrates claiming he was indeed in Athens at the time, and moreover that Hippocrates successfully cured the disease by lighting bonfires throughout Athens to purify the air. The legend is almost certainly apocryphal. To begin with, Thucydides writes explicitly that ancient doctors were ineffective at combating the plague. Moreover, the myriad documents that comprise the *Hippocratic Corpus* make no mention of the plague whatsoever, a glaring omission even if we accept that the *Corpus* is incomplete. But most importantly, this superficial idea of using fire to change the environment doesn't fit with any line of reasoning presented in the *Corpus*. The Hippocratic writers believed strongly that the environment both caused and affected disease, but don't write much about manipulating the environment, and certainly not on a massive scale. That said, a 1986 article by Prof. Jody Pinault in *The Journal of the History of Medicine and Allied Sciences* makes a compelling case for how and why the bonfire idea might have at least resonated with an ancient Greek doctor. The plan outlined by Hippocrates in chapter 22 are a nod to those arguments.

As to the other characters in the story, as a quick hint I've included family or place-of-origin names for true historical figures. Gorgias of Leontini was a renowned sophist who wrote and spoke in over-the-top, flowery rhetoric, as exemplified by his rather ludicrous *Encomium of Helen*. He's made somewhat of a fool by Socrates in Plato's Gorgias. If Plato can paint the man as something of a fool, why can't I? Democritus of Abdera was a 5th century BCE scientific philosopher that ancient sources name as a friend of Hippocrates. Phormio was one of the most successful Athenian generals during the time of the Peloponnesian War. And Cleon is the first genuine demagogue in recorded history that we're aware of. Thucydides is plainly disgusted with Cleon in the *History*, but it's in the plays of Aristophanes that Cleon is torn to pieces, with a mercilessness and hilarity that even the best of today's comedians would envy.

There is no evidence that Hippocrates was known to Socrates by anything other than reputation. I wrote their interaction in chapter 8 as a riff on Socrates' Social-Darwinist medical ethics – which would be considered abhorrent by modern standards – from Book III of Plato's *Republic*. While Socrates is immortal in the annals of Western thought, even in the fawning books of Plato he comes off as a pompous twit.

As to the female characters, none save Aspasia are named in the literature. Hippocrates was married, but his wife's name is nowhere to be found in the ancient sources. The assertion that Aristophanes married a one-time slave is my complete fiction, and an admittedly improbable one at that.

And if you were wondering, yes…Kleitos the "slack-jawed oaf", as he's referred to by Gorgias in chapter 4, is a shameless nod to the Cletus the Slack-Jawed Yokel from *The Simpsons*.

I've probably loved the culture and aesthetic of Ancient Greece since I saw the original *Clash of the Titans* movie. That's ironic, since 1) that movie retells a story from myth, not history, and 2) notwithstanding the awesome stop-motion visual effects, it gets enough of the Perseus story (intentionally?) wrong that it's a terrible replacement for literary sources. Even the best movie is no replacement for reading the damn book if you're a lazy grade 6 student.

Once I began exploring Classical Greece as an adult, though, I discovered that it remains one of the most fascinating periods of Western history. A big part of that is dumb luck – it's one of the few periods of ancient history for which we have an abundance of literary, artistic, and archeologic information, however incomplete that collection might be. Assuming culture might change but human nature does not, we can have a good sense of what daily life must have been like in ancient Athens in the 5th century BCE. .

Beyond the simple fact that we know a fair bit about Classical Greece, though, it's a society with a legacy of achievements that persist to this day. Full participatory democracy; popular jury courts; the Olympic games; scientific and moral philosophy; the study of argumentation and rhetoric; music theory; staged drama; fearless and bawdy comedy; and early scientific medicine all have their origins in ancient Greek society. The legends and great characters of Classical Greece echo in the 21st century. Our Iron Man and Avengers are their Jason and the Argonauts. Our Atul Gawande is their Hippocrates. Our Noam Chomsky is their Socrates. Our Sylvia Plath is their Sappho. Our Chris Rock and Jon Stewart are their Aristophanes. And our deep cultural devotion to the *Star Wars* and *Lord of the Rings* sagas approach their reverence for the legends of the Trojan War.

That's not to say Classical Greece should be blindly revered, but instead admired with eyes wide open. By our current standards, it was a society that bordered on awful to anyone apart from men of property. The status of women, even those born to noble families, was oppressive. Women were rarely provided an education, except those destined to become *hetaerae*, or courtesans. Marriage was a contract between a man and his future father-in-law, with the bride's wishes or interests given little or no thought. A bride, rarely past teenage years, was confined to the home to produce children – which was often fatal – and run the house while her husband served as breadwinner.

It's also impossible to ignore the fact that Classical Greece ran on slave labor. The monumental achievements we still enjoy today – the Parthenon, and ancient temples and theatres throughout the Greek countryside – were all built by slaves, using materials mined and quarried by slaves under punishing conditions few of us could imagine. The toil of slaves kept the ancient Greek citizens fed, freeing them up (or at least freeing the men) to engage in a dynamic political and intellectual life.

There's no end to our collective fascination with the ancient world, and I would direct readers to the massive list of artistic masterpieces and informative treatises out there, some already listed and almost all in the public domain. I turned to the Delphi Classics editions of Aristophanes, Euripides, Herodotus, Hippocrates, and Sappho, but that was simply for ease of use with an e-reader. All these works are freely available from the Gutenberg Project website or anywhere else that supplies books from the public domain, whether in digital or physical form. For summaries of the great myth stories, few books are as accessible as *Myths and Legends of Ancient Greece and Rome* by E.M. Berens. The Pope translations of Homer's *Iliad* and *Odyssey* are in rhyming verse, providing a sense of momentum and even fun when reading these timeless epics. *A Smaller History of Greece from the Earliest Times to the Roman Conquest* by William Smith gives a synopsis of the country's history and geography, offering details the ancient sources lack. And Aristotle's *The Athenian Constitution* offers a succinct history and structural description of the ancient Athenian government...required reading for political-historical junkies.

Dr. John Stewart Milne's 1907 *Surgical Instruments in Greek and Roman Times* is a gift to anyone reading or writing about ancient medicine, the perfect complement to *Outlines of Greek and Roman Medicine* by Sir James Sands Elliott. Galen's *On the Natural Faculties* does a better job describing the tenets of humorism than the *Hippocratic Corpus*, but Wikipedia works in a pinch.

For written descriptions of ancient Greek sailing vessels and triremes, I point the reader to Sir George Charles Vincent Holmes' *Ancient and Modern Ships, Part I: Wooden Sailing Ships*. And as someone who couldn't sail his way around or out of a bathtub, I relied on Admiral W.H. Smyth's *The Sailor's Word Book: An Alphabetical Digest of Nautical Terms*. As to the workings of ancient Greek metallurgy, the ultimate reference is *De Re Metallica*, translated from Latin by Georgius Agricola, but the processes used at Lavrion are better described by Prof. John Economopoulos in his 1996 article from *Mining History Journal*. For a wide-ranging discussion on the intersection between plague and Classical Athenian tragedy, see Prof. Robin Mitchell-Boyask's *Plague and the Athenian Imagination: Drama, History, and the Cult of Asclepius*.

I would be remiss if I didn't point to my favorite source on all things related to Classical Greece: the offerings and professors of The Great Courses. I've worked my way through dozens of Great Courses series, on everything from quantum physics to art appreciation to complex systems theory to the history of jazz, but this book owes a great deal to the following series:

First and foremost, *Peloponnesian War* by Prof. Kenneth Harl and *Age of Pericles* by Prof. Jeremy McInerney. These two series complement one another perfectly and give as much detail as you could ever want around the complex history and daily lives of ancient Athenians at the time of the Peloponnesian War. They are must-have courses for Classical history buffs.

If you prefer a broad overview to deep historical detail, Prof. Rufus Fears is a terrific storyteller in *Famous Greeks*. Prof. Robert Garland offers *The Other Side of History: Daily Life in the Ancient World*, and the book I leaned on heavily while writing this one, *Ancient Greece: Everyday Life in the Birthplace of Western Civilization*. Prof. John Hale's *Great Tours: Greece and Turkey, from Athens to Istanbul* takes you on a guided visual tour of the important locations in ancient Greece, offering a ton of historical anecdotes and insights to boot. I would not have a clue about Gorgias or his teachings – some of the most fun parts of the book to write – without

Prof. Michael Sugrue's *Plato, Socrates, and the Dialogues*. Prof. Elizabeth Vandiver's *Classical Mythology* gives the background on the stories that underlie ancient Greek culture, and *Greek Tragedy* describes how those stories were staged for, and likely resonated with, a live audience. Last but most assuredly not least, the series taught by Prof. Stephen Ressler are simply flawless in both content and presentation. I can't recommend his courses *Understanding Greek and Roman Technology: From Catapult to the Pantheon* and *Understanding the World's Greatest Structures: Science and Innovation from Antiquity to Modernity* highly enough.

Writing a work of fiction about someone as important to medical history as Hippocrates is a humbling undertaking. As anyone familiar with my first book or social media posts can attest, I can't even try to measure up to him as a doctor, never mind as a revolutionary of medical science with a legacy measured in millennia. But as a doctor myself, I'm one of his countless disciples by default. I hope I've done his name honor in crafting this story, and I hope you've enjoyed the experience in reading it. It was simply a joy to research and put together.

ACKNOWLEDGEMENTS

Whether an author wants to admit it or not, writing a book is not a solo exercise. I owe a great deal of thanks to some brilliant and extraordinary professionals that donated their time, scholarly thought, and vital feedback to help make this book a reality.

Thanks to Dr. Robert Garland for his exhaustive review of the manuscript for historical accuracy, providing substantive feedback on the book's dramatic climax, and giving me an exclusive sneak peak at his own creative projects.

Thanks to Dr. Jeremy McInerney, for correcting small historical details not found in the sources.

Thanks to Dr. Susan Nasif, for ensuring my science was at the very least plausible.

Thanks to Dr. Paul Dhillon and Dr. Jon Johnsen, for honest critique and excellent editorial feedback.

Thanks to Ben and Chloe, the greatest kids in the world.

And my deepest, most enduring love and thanks to Dr. Kylea Potvin, for believing in me and keeping me around, what with the insurance riding on my head and all.

ABOUT THE AUTHOR

Dr. Franklin Warsh is an Investigating Coroner and retired Family Doctor from Toronto, Canada. He is a regular contributor to Canada's *Medical Post*, and the author of a professional memoir, *The Flame Broiled Doctor: From Boyhood to Burnout in Medicine*. His website and blog on all things related to health care and medicine can be found at http://drwarsh.blogspot.com.

Frank now lives in "the other London", Canada, alongside his wife, children, and profoundly sedentary pets. If he can steal time away from the laptop, laundry, and lunchmaking, he's probably caught in a daydream.